"Rumor Has It You're Engaged," Gui's Friend Tristan Said.

"Yes," Gui said. He would have to convince Kara that the engagement was real for now. No way would he expose her to society's snide comments, by admitting that a moment of weakness had made him claim her as his own.

"Kara's a good choice for you."

"She is?" He knew nothing about the woman except that she had the softest lips he'd ever tasted. When he kissed her, he forgot that all other women existed.

Not a bad start for an affair, but marriage… Damn. Was he really considering marrying her?

As his friend's words echoed in his mind, he realized that, yes, he was.

Dear Reader,

When I started thinking about writing foreign heroes, a man popped immediately into my head—Antonio Banderas. He's sexy and funny and speaks with that lovely Spanish accent. Lusting over a picture isn't enough to make a story, but it was a nice start.

Because Guillermo is an aristocrat, I read up on the different European royals. The idea for his story is based on the Charles-Diana-Camilla triangle, which I twisted so that Gui missed his chance with the woman he *thought* he loved. He decided never to marry. Enter Kara.

Kara is a heroine who's close to my heart. My entire life, I've had body issues and have always felt too big no matter what size I am. I was looking at the little girls at my son's elementary school and realized that, when you're their age, you feel like a princess. You don't realize that society wants princesses to be one size (tiny) and that you might not fit the mold. And Kara came out of that. She's the nice sister, the fat sister, the reliable sister (all things I am by the way!), but not the pretty one.

Gui has three sisters and truly loves all women in all their forms. When he sees Kara, he sees her loveliness and that she's not like her sister. I had a lot of fun writing this book and doing research on Madrid. I'm dying to go there. I hope you enjoy *The Spanish Aristocrat's Woman!*

Happy reading!

Katherine

KATHERINE GARBERA

THE SPANISH ARISTOCRAT'S WOMAN

Published by Silhouette Books
America's Publisher of Contemporary Romance

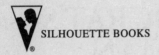

SILHOUETTE BOOKS

ISBN-13: 978-0-373-76858-5
ISBN-10:   0-373-76858-3

THE SPANISH ARISTOCRAT'S WOMAN

Copyright © 2008 by Katherine Garbera

Books by Katherine Garbera

Silhouette Desire

†*His Wedding-Night Wager* #1708
†*Her High-Stakes Affair* #1714
†*Their Million-Dollar Night* #1720
The Once-a-Mistress Wife #1749
**Make-Believe Mistress* #1798
**Six-Month Mistress* #1802
**High-Society Mistress* #1808
The Greek Tycoon's Secret Heir #1845
The Wealthy Frenchman's Proposition #1851
The Spanish Aristocrat's Woman #1858

Silhouette Bombshell

Exposed #10
Night Life #23
The Amazon Strain #43
Exclusive #94

†What Happens in Vegas…
**The Mistresses
*Sons of Privilege

KATHERINE GARBERA

is a strong believer in happily-ever-after. She's written more than thirty-five books and has been nominated for *Romantic Times BOOKreviews* career achievement awards in Series Fantasy and Series Adventure. Her books have appeared on the Waldenbooks bestseller list for series romance and on the *USA TODAY* extended bestseller list. Visit Katherine on the Web at www.katherinegarbera.com.

This book is dedicated to the friends who have helped me through the last year. I didn't realize until my world was crumbling how stalwart your friendship was. So big thanks and much love to Rob, Eve, Beverly, Janet, Lenora, Denise and Franny.

Acknowledgments

I have to say thank you to my editor, Natashya Wilson, who always manages to get what I was trying to say and make my books stronger.

One

It was being billed as the wedding of the year—the union of Manhattan's most romantic couple. And as far as Kara deMontaine could see, the media was right on the money with this one. She stood in the back of the packed Saint Patrick's Cathedral surrounded by society's elite. This was her world, her circle. And yet, she felt totally alone as she waited to be escorted down the aisle to her seat.

The unexpected wedding of publishing magnate Tristan Sabina had turned into *the* event of the spring season. She wished she could look at it as just another party, but she was almost thirty and still single. So every wedding she attended was turning into a trial, a kind of endurance event that made her realize she was probably never going to be a bride. She tried to shake off the melancholy that seemed to wrap around her like an Hermès silk scarf. But she couldn't.

It had nothing to do with Sheri Donnelly, the bride. Kara knew little about her, but she had heard that Sheri was very sweet. She'd also heard a first-hand account from her older sister, Rina, that Sheri's dress was one-of-a-kind exquisite.

Kara felt a longing that she'd been unable to shake lately. That longing to wear a white dress. To see her groom, standing at the end of the aisle waiting for her. To walk through a church filled with onlookers all envious of her, because on this one day she was the most beautiful woman in the world.

She felt the sting of tears in her eyes as she remembered lying in bed with her mother on lazy Sunday mornings and talking about her dream wedding. Rina always curled up on the right side and Kara on the left in her parents' king-sized bed. Back then she hadn't realized that she wasn't a fairy-tale princess. Hadn't realized that being almost six feet tall and big boned would make most men a little hesitant around her.

She closed her eyes and heard the sweet, soft voice of her mother as nothing more than a dream.

Alisha deMontaine had died when Kara was six-teen, just before she was to make her rounds as a debutante. Rina had made her debut a year earlier.

Rina and Kara were as opposite as two women could be. Where Rina was petite, thin and revered for her beauty, Kara was tall, a bit on the solid side and known for her charitable work.

Kara sniffed and blinked rapidly, knowing that, while it was okay to cry when the bride appeared, sobbing before the event started would be a major faux pas.

A hand fell on her shoulder and a snowy white handkerchief appeared in front of her eyes. The hand holding it was tanned, masculine and very large.

"A wedding day is a day of joy," the man said in a deep, strong voice with a thick Spanish accent.

She glanced up into hazel eyes. He was stun-ningly handsome and staring at her with concentra-tion. He was also taller than her, which made him about six-two or six-three. She cleared her throat and quickly wiped her eyes. "Tears of joy."

He quirked one eyebrow at her. And there was something arrogant in the way he did it. "I know women."

No doubt. He exuded a blatant sexuality that probably drew more women to his side than he wanted. Then again, he looked as though he was more than able to handle any situation, even a flock of women descending on him. Okay, she was getting a little hysterical. She took a deep breath. Poise was something she was known for. It was time to find it. Time to get control.

"You might know women," she said, "but you don't know me."

He nodded. "Let's change that. I am Count Guillermo de Cuaron y Bautista de la Cruz. And you are?"

She knew who he was. He was in the tabloids all the time for his escapades around the world. And Rina traveled on the outskirts of his circle of friends.

Guillermo always had a beautiful woman on his arm. Never a pudgy heiress like her. Dang it, she was trying to be more comfortable in the size-twelve body that she had. Nothing could get her down to a zero. *Nothing*. She'd dieted more times than she wanted to admit.

"Kara deMontaine," she said, holding her hand out to him.

He took it and brushed his lips across the back of her hand. "Now that we are no longer strangers…what has you teary eyed on this happy day?"

She shook her head. Yeah, like she was really going to tell this stunningly gorgeous man that she was upset because she was never going to be a picture-perfect bride. "You wouldn't understand."

"Try me."

"Count—"

"My friends call me Gui."

"Gui," she said without meaning to. She liked the way his name sounded on her lips. And she loved his voice. The accent made her want to listen to him all day.

"Kara, tell me. I have three sisters and numerous cousins. I'm a good listener."

There was something very kind and understanding in his eyes. She wanted to pour out the entire sad truth. That she'd probably never marry like this. Never find a man to cherish her. Never be a bride envied by the world. But she couldn't say those words out loud to this man. He was handsome, actually almost beautiful with his classical features, dark blond hair and multihued eyes. A fantasy man, and she was a married-for-her-money kind of girl. "It's a silly thing."

"Ah, that means it is actually a very personal thought. Something that means a lot to you," he said.

God, she didn't want him to be perceptive enough to know what was really bothering her. She had made her peace with who she was and how she looked, and that worked for her only because everyone believed she was happy living in Rina's shadow. And most days, she was. "Please don't."

"Don't what?"

"Don't try to pretend you really care what I have to say or what upset me. I know I'm the last woman you'd normally look at."

He drew her out of the crowded foyer of the church and off to a quiet hallway. She loved the cathedral. Even though her family wasn't Catholic, she'd been to the church a lot just to walk around and study the architecture.

"What do you know of me? Were we not just introduced?" he asked.

She blushed, thinking of all the stories she'd heard about him. Tristan she'd known for ages, because his sister, Blanche, and her sister were best friends. So she knew stories of Gui, Tristan and Christos. She'd heard about Seconds, the clubs they co-owned together, and about their wild parties, and had seen with her own envious eyes the beautiful women who always surrounded them.

"I'm Rina's sister," she said, as if that would explain it all.

"Ah. Well, what did Rina tell you about me?" he asked.

Rina protected Kara as if she were her mother. She'd warned Kara to stay away from men like Guillermo. Men who were too confident in how they looked and their ability to win over any woman.

"Just that… Listen, can you please just let this go?"

"No."

"No?"

"I think it means the same thing in practically every language, *querida*."

"I'm not your darling," she said through clenched teeth, hating the fact that she'd always been emotional and cried so easily. If not for that, Guillermo would never have noticed her and she wouldn't be having this conversation.

"Why does that make you defensive?" he asked.

"Count—"

"Gui," he said. "I'm not going to let this go."

She shook her head. "Why do you care?"

"Because you look so sad. I want to make you smile."

"Make me smile?" she asked, unable to believe he really would. "I'm the fat sister. *The nice sister.* The one no one pays any attention to."

Gui stroked one finger down the side of her face, running lightly over a cheekbone and the line of her jaw. "You are exquisite, Kara. Not fat at all. Why do you believe this?"

"Because I look in the mirror before I leave the house."

"Maybe your mirror is distorted," he said.

His hand cupped her face and she caught her breath at the way he touched her. It was almost as if he was compelled to. "No. Don't be silly."

He shook his head. "Tell me what made you cry."

"Nothing in particular. I was just staring at this lovely venue and thinking about the bride."

"Sheri and Tristan are meant to be together," he said. "Did you love him?"

"*No*. Tristan has always treated me like a little sister. And I've never thought of him that way." She was horrified that anyone would think she was crying because she'd been in love with the groom.

"Then why?" he asked again.

She took a deep breath, knowing she was going to tell him, if only to stop this crazy conversation. But she couldn't while he was touching her or looking at her. She took his hand in her own and pressed his handkerchief to his palm.

"Because I'll never be that kind of bride."

She walked away from him, because she did have some pride. And there was something compelling about Guillermo de la Cruz that made her want to tell him all of the secrets she usually kept buried down deep inside her soul.

With her long, thick black hair, olive skin and exotic eyes, Elvira looked like a Mediterranean sex goddess as she sat at the center of a table surrounded by her crowd of admirers. Gui would like to think he wasn't one of them, but he refused to lie to himself and Elvira had always been his weakness.

The fact that he'd resisted her charms since she'd married his old friend Juan was something he prided himself on, but he did still lust after her. And as a Catholic, he knew that sin in thought was just as bad as sin in the flesh.

Rumors had always abounded about him and Elvira, despite the fact that he'd tried to keep his distance. There was something about her that drew his attention, and his interest never went unnoticed by the tabloids.

Gui glanced around the reception, which was being held at the most fashionable hotel in Manhattan. In a while he'd be stepping up to give the toast to Sheri and Tristan, and he should be concentrating on that. Instead, he was fixated on a woman—Elvira. He'd been obsessed with her since he was eighteen.

"See something you like?"

He glanced over at Christos, who'd come up next to him and was handing him a glass of champagne. Christos had recently married as well. And though the institution had always been one Gui dreaded, he had to admit that his friend looked happier than he had in years. In fact, if pressed, Gui would be forced to say that marriage had changed Christos for the better.

"Yes."

"Which one?" Christos asked.

Gui knew better than to admit he'd been watching Elvira, so he skimmed the crowd and spotted Kara deMontaine.

"Um…tall, thick curly hair…" he said.

"Ah, the younger deMontaine girl. Kerri?"

"Kara. Do you know her?"

"Not well. I do know Rina fairly well. She's very protective of the girl."

"Really?"

"Yes. She tore someone to shreds once for a comment they made about her."

Gui said nothing, just took a sip of his drink, pretending he was unable to take his eyes off Kara. Her hair *was* thick and black, and it curled around her face like a Botticelli angel's. She was tall, at least five-ten. And her figure was full. Her curves were generous, but she could never be called fat. He'd been sincere when he'd complimented her. She wasn't a classically beautiful woman like Elvira, and she'd never draw men to her the way that his ex-lover did, but there was an innocence about Kara that was refreshing.

"Gui?"

"Hmm?" Gui tried not to dwell on the fact that he actually was having trouble taking his eyes off Kara.

"You okay?" Christos asked.

"Why wouldn't I be? Weddings are a single man's best friend." The band was playing a lively number. And he was going to find a single woman to go home with him tonight. Not Elvira. And not an innocent like Kara.

"No reason," Christos said.

"You are being vague. What's up?" It wasn't like Christos to beat around the bush.

"Ava thinks you are…"

"What?" he asked, distracted. "What are you getting at?"

"Ah, hell, I feel stupid even saying it."

"Just say it."

"She thinks that with Tristan and I both married, you're going to feel isolated."

Gui smiled. Ava Niarchos was a deeply caring and compassionate woman. And she worried over Christos's friends as if they were her own. She'd told him at Tristan's engagement party that she wanted him and Tristan settled down, so that Christos, Tristan and he could raise families together.

But in all honesty, that wasn't a lifestyle that Gui wanted. "I'm not isolated. You and Tristan are my mates and that's not going to change because you're married."

Christos rubbed the back of his neck. "I told you—"

"*Amigo,* it's okay. I understand. Tell Ava thank you for worrying about me."

"She'd worry less if the rumors about you and Elvira would go away."

"She's worried about Elvira?" he asked, wondering how Ava had even heard the other woman's name. Probably the tabloids, which were Sheri's favorite vice. Sheri and Ava had become close.

Christos shrugged.

"I am not interested in married women. You know I take vows seriously."

"Indeed. So why are you looking at her when you think no one will notice?"

"I'm not."

"Juan is watching you like he's going to confront you."

"Where is he?"

"The bar."

Juan couldn't handle his liquor. He'd been asked to leave events at the Spanish Court before. Gui's sister-in-law, Dulcinea, the Enfanta, was worried about Juan, who was her first cousin.

"I'm not looking at Elvira more than I am any other woman."

"Gui—"

"Christos, I've never interfered in your personal life."

Christos snorted. "So when you showed up on Mykonos to meet Ava before our wedding, that wasn't interfering?" Gui shrugged, and Christos laughed. "I'll leave it be. Just watch your back."

Gui nodded and walked away from Christos, trying to remember that his life was a happy one. He wasn't like Tristan, who'd mourned the death of his first love for too long before meeting Sheri, or like Christos, who had felt betrayed by the woman he loved before they worked out their differences.

He was a bachelor. He liked the lifestyle and the women. He'd learned long ago that a man with passions like his was better suited to short-term relationships.

The one woman he'd opened his heart to had married out of spite to make him jealous, and Gui had learned the hard way that love wasn't all hearts and flowers. Love was also painful and vindictive.

He glanced at the bar, catching Juan's glare. He needed to do something. Anything that would make Juan believe that he wasn't still attracted to Elvira. It didn't help matters that at some point, Elvira would seek him out. She always did. And he always waited for her.

"Care to dance?"

Kara had a light buzz going from all the pomegranate martinis she'd drunk. She was surrounded by her friends and really enjoying herself. And those were good enough reasons for asking Gui to dance.

Those, and the fact that her friend Courtney had been certain that Kara didn't know him. Didn't really know the gorgeous and most sought-after bachelor in the room.

"Pardon?"

She cleared her throat. Man, if he turned her down, she was going to die. "I asked you to dance."

"Dance?"

"Unless there is something official you should be doing."

"I have a few moments. Enough time to dance with a beautiful woman." He smiled at her, his expression very charming. "It would be my pleasure to dance with you."

She flushed as a totally inappropriate thought drifted through her mind. Then she shook her head and led him to the dance floor and her group of friends. "Do you know everyone?"

He shook his head. "Hello, ladies."

Kara introduced him to Emily, Katie and Courtney. They were her best friends and some of the only people she was truly comfortable around.

"This is Count…Gui. I'm sorry I don't remember your entire title."

He smiled at that. "I'm Count Guillermo de Cuaron y Bautista de la Cruz. But please, just Gui."

He bowed and the girls all dropped into low curtsies as they'd been taught long ago. Gui smiled at them and Katie giggled.

The music changed from lively to a slow ballad. Kara started edging her way off the dance floor but Gui stopped her with his hand on her arm.

"I believe you asked me to dance."

"Yes," she said.

He drew her back toward the center of the dance floor and into his arms. Even in her heels he was taller than she was. He smoothed his hands down her back, resting them just above the curve of her hips.

He was a good dancer, which made sense. He owned several nightclubs and had probably spent a fair amount of time frequenting the trendy nightspots. Each with a different woman.

She sighed. Why had her thoughts turned to that?

"What are you thinking?"

She shook her head. There weren't enough martinis in this room to get her to admit what she'd been thinking. "Nothing."

"You sighed."

"I did."

"So…"

"Gui?"

"Yes, Kara."

"Stop being charming."

He laughed and lifted his head. "I can't. It's a curse of mine."

"And you use it very well."

"You say that as if it were a bad thing."

"Well, it makes you seem like the kind of man who always knows the right thing to say."

"Fake?" he asked.

She bit her lower lip. "Yes. Fake. I mean, you say things to me that sound like you really care, but you hardly know me."

"Perhaps you're easier to care about than you think."

She shook her head. "I know I'm not. No man ever sees me as anything other than an heiress."

"Then they aren't really looking at you," Guillermo said.

Kara felt something shift inside her as she looked at Gui. He drew her even more closely to him until her breasts brushed his chest and her head rested on his shoulder.

She feared this was a martini-induced dream, but it felt incredibly real to her and she wanted it to last for a little while longer. Tomorrow she could go back to being the pudgy heiress. Tonight, she wanted to revel in the feeling of being a fairy-tale princess with her count.

"Guillermo, *querido?*"

The voice was low and husky and very feminine. And there was a hint of possessiveness in that voice as its owner spoke to Gui.

He stiffened and his features tightened, but she didn't know him well enough to really read his reaction. "*Si,* Elvira."

"Introduce me to your lovely friend," the woman named Elvira said.

Kara heard the criticism in the other woman's voice. That note that said, why are you dancing with this pudgy girl instead of me? It was a tone that Kara had heard often enough over the years.

"Countess Elvira de Castillo y Perez, meet Kara deMontaine. Kara, this is the Countess Elvira."

"It's a pleasure to meet you," Kara said, curtsying to the older woman.

"Aren't you a sweet child," the countess said.

"Run along and play with your friends. I'd like a word with Guillermo."

Kara started to step away but Gui's hand tightened on her arm. "Kara is my fiancée, Elvira. Anything you have to say to me can be said in front of her."

TWO

Kara smiled politely but inside her mind was reeling. What the hell was Gui thinking? She started to speak but he bent to her and brushed his lips over hers.

She parted hers in surprise and felt the brush of his tongue against hers. Then it was gone. "I'm sorry, Elvira, we don't have time to chat. I promised this dance to Kara."

Gui danced her away from the other woman. And she just stared up at him, for the first time in her life completely unsure of what to do next.

"Um…"

"Don't say anything just yet. Dance with me and look up at me the way a woman in love would."

"And how is that?"

"With adoration, of course."

She had to smile at him. And he leaned down to once again touch his mouth to hers. She opened her mouth this time, hoping to taste him again. That first kiss had been too quick, too brief, and it left her wanting more of him.

He angled his head and his tongue touched hers. She breathed into his mouth and felt the contact of his lips and tongue on hers all the way to her core. Chills raced down her body, making her breasts feel fuller and her nipples harden.

She pulled back from him and held tightly on to his shoulders, having the very real feeling that she was in way over her head. This was different than asking a cute guy to dance…this was passion.

Something that had always been lacking in her life.

"Gui…"

"Kara. You have the most kissable lips."

She shook her head. Her mouth tingled. Tingled! She wanted to touch her lips but knew she'd give away just how inexperienced she was to him.

"Trust me," he said, bending down to take her mouth one more time. She shivered in his arms. She knew the music changed, because the couples around them seemed to be moving, but time stood still for her as she stood there with Gui. As she felt the warmth of his big body next to hers. The way he wrapped his arms around her waist and let his hands drift lower to cup her buttocks and draw her more fully into his body.

She melted against him. For the first time she felt like one of those delicate girls she'd always envied. In Gui's arms she wasn't too big. She didn't tower over him. And when he touched her, his hands were strong and sure.

She pulled back, afraid that she was losing her perspective, and looked up into his warm hazel eyes. But they weren't the same light brown-green they'd been earlier. Now they were stormy with a bit of gray moving in around the rims of his irises.

"Your eyes," she said, raising one hand to trace his eyebrow.

"What about them?"

"They're changing color."

He quirked an eyebrow, the one she wasn't touching, at her.

"They were this light earth tone…like a spring lake…earlier, but now there's more gray in them… like the Northern Atlantic Ocean."

"Do you like the water, *querida?*"

He was calling her darling again. She told herself it was probably an affectation, something he did with every woman, but it didn't stop the little thrill from going through her each time he said it.

"I love it," she said. In the water it didn't matter that she was taller and bigger than everyone else. She felt svelte and slim.

"Do you sail?" he asked.

"Yes. I just ordered a new yacht," she said. "I'm picking it up in Monte Negro soon."

"I love Monte Negro," Gui said, stroking one finger down the side of her face. "Why there?"

"One of my cousins took a job there. I am going to Italy in a few weeks with a group of inner-city teenagers who are interested in fashion design."

"Fashion?"

She pulled away. "I know I might not seem like the right woman to guide them—"

"I wasn't questioning your fashion sense. You're incredibly beautiful in this dress. It's just not often that I hear about fashion design programs for the underprivileged."

"That's precisely why I did it. I have a program for plus-sized girls, too. I hate the way that fashion magazines and the fashion industry just focus on skinny women."

She put her hand over her mouth. That comment

was way too revealing. Why were they talking about her? She should be demanding to know why he'd said she was his fiancée.

"We need to talk, Gui."

"I know, *querida*."

"Please call me Kara. I don't like being called by a generic endearment."

"*Querida* isn't generic when it's applied to you," he said.

But he must use it for Elvira. Because she'd called him *querido,* which was the masculine version of that endearment. "All the same."

"You aren't what I expected."

"Why would I be?" she asked. "You don't know me at all."

"Well, *mi dulce,* I think that's going to change rather quickly."

"Why do you think that? Because we're 'engaged'?" she asked.

She heard a gasp and turned around to look down into the face of her sister, Rina.

"You're *engaged* to Count Guillermo?"

Gui hadn't thought through his rash words to Elvira. His only thought had been to change the dynamic that had existed between the two of them for more than a decade. She'd had all the power. He was insanely jealous and, because of his own views on infidelity, powerless to change anything.

But saying that Kara was his fiancée had given him a glimpse of change. Elvira's eyes had narrowed and he knew that he'd finally jarred her from that safe position she'd held over him for years.

Of course, he didn't intend to marry a woman he hardly knew. But seeing the blood drain from Kara's face as her sister asked if they were engaged…well, he couldn't just walk away from her. His father was big on personal responsibility, and walking away from a woman in a situation like this wasn't something he could do.

He wrapped his arm around Kara and drew her more fully against the side of his body. Rina was a beautiful woman and, seeing the way she regarded him now, he realized Christos had been right when he'd said that she was very protective of her little sister.

"Well, it's been a secret until now, Rina. We didn't want to steal any of Sheri and Tristan's day," Gui said.

Kara looked up at him and he could see the panic rising in her. He was used to managing people and taking control of situations and he did exactly that now. "Right, Kara?"

She nodded and tried to smile but failed miserably.

"You okay?" Rina asked Kara.

"I'm fine. Really. I just didn't expect anyone to hear about this…"

"Does Dad know?"

Their father was on the West Coast, closing a business deal, and hadn't been able to make the wedding.

"No."

Rina nodded. "Let's go someplace quiet so we can talk."

"I'm sorry, Rina, but we're already committed to joining Christos and Ava after this dance. I'm making the wedding toast. We'll see you later."

"We're available for breakfast, Rina," Kara said.

Gui squeezed her arm in warning. He didn't want to dine with her sister and field questions to which he had no answers.

Kara tipped her head to the side and gave him a level stare. "*Querido,* you said that you'd always have time for my family."

"Of course, I did."

He needed to get Kara alone to talk to her. Seriously. Until he laid some ground rules, she was going to run amok saying whatever she wanted to. And he was going to have to agree.

"I guess I'll see you tomorrow morning. Nine?" Rina asked.

"Sounds good," Kara said.

Gui cupped her elbow and led her off the dance floor and out of the reception ballroom. The hotel lobby was filled with gawkers who weren't invited to the reception and who were hanging out, hoping for a glimpse of the glamorous wedding guests.

He was always relatively incognito in the States because he was a lesser royal from Spain. In Europe he would have been mobbed, but here he wasn't.

"Where are we going?" Kara asked. She tried to slow their pace, but Gui kept his arm around her waist and forced her to keep moving forward.

"Somewhere where we can be alone, *mi dulce*."

"Gui," she said, flat-out stopping.

"Si?"

"This is getting out of hand."

"No, it's not," he said. In his entire life, there'd been nothing he couldn't manage and make work to his advantage.

He knew this "engagement" wasn't the smartest thing he'd ever gotten himself into, but he was confident he'd be able to think of something that would get the both of them out of it.

"I think it is. I've never been engaged before. I'm almost thirty and chubby and everyone knows that the only reason men are interested in me is the fortune I bring with me."

Gui shook his head. "Almost thirty isn't a curse.

I'm nearly forty. You're not chubby, and I don't want to hear you refer to yourself that way again. You are a goddess among women—"

"Don't lie to me about my body," she said, interrupting him. "I've been this size for most of my life and know I'm not a goddess."

Gui nudged her out of the main traffic path and into a nearly deserted hallway. She spun to face him and pressed back against the wall. He put his hands on either side of her head and leaned in close, so close that he felt the exhalation of her breath against his cheek.

Her eyes were wide as she gazed up at him. There were doubts and insecurity in her eyes. He was suddenly angry at all of his sex for allowing any woman to feel unattractive because of something as silly as height and weight.

"Kara, *mi dulce,* I'm not a man who says things because I think they will win me favor. I do know how to be charming, I'm not going to deny that, but you should know right now that when I say something to you, I'm not lying."

"All I know is that I've always been too big to be really fashionable and—"

He leaned down and brushed his lips over her forehead and then dropped a few soft kisses on her lips. He pulled back and looked down at her.

"You are certainly not like anyone else. You are an Amazon goddess. Your skin is so smooth and soft, I can't get enough of touching it."

"Yeah, but I'm too tall," she said.

"For other men, perhaps, but for me you are a perfect fit," he said, drawing her into his arms. Her head rested comfortably on his shoulder.

He didn't let himself dwell on the sweetness he felt toward her. It was unlike anything he'd felt for any woman. With Elvira, he felt passion and jealousy. And he doted on his sisters, but this affection—and passion—that he felt for Kara seemed so different.

He had no idea what it meant. He'd used her as a weapon in his private war with Elvira. To show the other woman that she no longer had the power to make him insanely jealous. Which had led to this current insanity.

"Gui?"

"Hmm?"

"Why are you looking at me like that?"

"Like what?"

She shrugged. "Never mind. Are we going to talk here?"

"No. But we aren't moving until you acknowledge that you are an attractive woman."

* * *

Kara had never had any man watch her the way Gui did, as if he were starving and she was the only thing that looked good. A part of her—okay, all of her—wanted to believe him when he said she was beautiful. But the only man to ever really make her believe he thought she was more than a big girl was her father. And that was because she felt confident that he loved her.

Now she was standing in an open and public place and this very attractive man was leaning over her, wanting her to accept…that she was more than she knew she was.

She could lie and say whatever he wanted—but she would never do that.

"I can't say something I don't believe," she said at last, knowing that much about herself.

Usually she had no trouble dismissing men's insincere flattery. But with Gui…what would be the reason to lie to her? He didn't need her fortune or her connections. From the rumors she'd heard about him, his fortune far exceeded her own. And he was the brother-in-law of the Enfanta—his older brother was married to the royal princess of Spain.

"Why don't you believe me?" he asked, stroking a finger down the side of her face.

She shrugged. Surely he didn't want her to point

out in detail every thing that was wrong with her. She'd probably start crying, and she'd already cried once in front of him.

"Suffice it to say, I'm into truth in a big way."

"Maybe it's because I am not American, but I do not understand your meaning."

She wasn't going to explain. She did have some pride, and telling this man about the insecurities she'd always carried with her wasn't something she wanted to do.

Figuring out this engagement problem was something else. Rina wasn't going to settle for evasions or half-truths. And Kara couldn't lie to Rina anyway.

"Guillermo?"

"Yes, *querida?*"

She still didn't like hearing that endearment from him. It was one he used without thought. And true, they barely knew each other, but she didn't want to be one of a crowd to him.

Oh no, she was already falling for him.

"You are frowning. Have I said something to offend you?"

She tried to move away from him but he had positioned his body in such a way that she was trapped. Caught between him and the wall, but to a larger extent caught between who she'd always been and who she wished she could be.

That was the real danger. Gui made her feel that she wasn't the overweight heiress she'd always been. Instead, she felt like a woman. A feminine and attractive woman, wanted by a very sexy man.

"Tell me."

She became flustered and unsure of what to say to him. She really didn't want to be one of the faceless masses of women who flocked around him, but at the same time, she was leery of saying the wrong thing and driving him away.

Oh, man. She had it bad. A little masculine attention, and she was turning into one of those silly airheads that she and her friends usually disdained.

"Kara, I'm waiting."

God, he was arrogant and bossy. She wanted to pretend it bothered her, but a part of her liked the way he demanded things from her. Demanded that she tell him what she felt as if he really cared about what was going on inside her head. Even his caresses felt like demands, and not in a bad way at all.

"As I said before, I don't like being called by a generic endearment. Something you call every woman."

His eyes blazed into hers. "Then I won't call you that anymore."

"Count de Cuaron, I'd like a word with you."

Gui stiffened and Kara looked over his shoulder to see a man of Spanish descent coming toward them. Gui cursed under his breath and turned.

"Not now, Juan."

"Yes, now." Juan's accent was much heavier than Gui's, and Kara could almost feel the animosity coming off of him in waves.

Gui blocked her body with his own. He said something in Spanish in a very low voice. She couldn't make out all the words, but she did hear the name *Elvira*. All the good feelings she'd had in his arms evaporated.

She'd never really paid much attention to the European social set apart from whatever affected Rina. But now she wished she had. Because it was clear that whatever was between Gui and Elvira hadn't sprung up yesterday but had been lingering for a long time.

Juan, whoever he was, was clearly in the middle between Gui and the other woman.

She could handle the humiliation of telling her sister she wasn't really engaged to Gui. But she couldn't handle being used. And it was clear to her that, whatever was going on with Gui, he'd had entirely selfish reasons for making that ridiculous comment about them being engaged.

No matter what she looked like or what she'd always believed about herself, Kara had always had one thing that was hers and hers alone. And that was confidence that she deserved better than to be used either for her money or her station, or, in this case, because she was convenient.

While his attention was on the other man, she ducked under Gui's arm and started to walk away.

Three

The last thing that Gui wanted to deal with at this moment was Juan. He no longer could tolerate his cousin by marriage. The man had been a friend when they'd been children. But as an adult he'd turned into Elvira's lapdog.

He knew that she'd married Juan in part because Gui and Juan had at one time been friends. That was the kind of woman Elvira was. Preying on a man's weakness.

"Excuse me, Count. I really should be returning to the reception," Kara said, ducking under his arm.

He snagged her wrist and held her in place by his

side. "We both should. Juan, whatever you need will have to wait."

"I'm not—"

"I'm afraid you are," Gui said, talking over Juan's protest. "Call my assistant and schedule an appointment if we need to meet."

Juan narrowed his eyes and for a moment Gui wondered if his old friend was finally finding his backbone. He drew Kara back to his side and positioned himself slightly in front of her body in case Juan decided to do something stupid.

"I will do that. We really need to talk."

Juan stalked away and Kara tugged on her hand. He lifted it to his mouth and kissed the back of it gently. "I'm sorry, *mi dulce.*"

"Sorry? Sorry doesn't work in this case, Guillermo. You can't keep me by your side when I want to leave."

He lifted her shackled wrist and arched one eyebrow at her. He knew he was being arrogant, but no one told him what to do. And when it came to women he'd always gotten his way. Why should Kara be any different?

She tugged again on her wrist. And he held her in a loose but secure grip.

"A man who has to resort to this type of action to keep a woman by his side isn't much of a man."

He pulled her off balance and into his arms, dropping her wrist as his mouth came down on hers, a hard slash that established his dominance over her.

Immediately he lessened the intensity of the kiss, wanting to show her that he didn't need to use force to keep a woman by his side. As soon as he did she softened against him. Her arms went around his waist and she tipped her head to the side, giving him greater access to her mouth.

She sighed when he pulled back and Gui looked down at her. She was different from any other woman he'd kissed. As all women essentially were, but this time with Kara—she was really different. Her tongue moistened her lips. She opened her eyes, her gaze meeting his, and he forgot that he'd been proving a point. All he wanted to do was taste her again. Tease them both into forgetting that they were essentially strangers.

He lowered his head and touched the tip of her tongue with his. She drew his lower lip between her tongue and teeth and suckled on him.

He groaned deep in his throat. She clung to him, and he felt the passion rising in her body. He tamped down on his own urges, reaching deep to control the need to savage her mouth and then take her against the wall.

"Gui?" she asked, her voice low and dreamy.

"Hmm?" How easily he could claim this woman as his. There was a vulnerability in her eyes that he could exploit, and with another woman he might not hesitate to do it, to use her in his private war with Elvira. Although that's what he'd done earlier, when he'd announced their engagement, now his intentions were changing.

He saw beyond a pawn in the game that had gone on too long to the woman here in his arms. A woman that he knew he didn't want to hurt. He rubbed his thumb over her full lower lip, tracing it lightly until she shivered delicately in his arms and smiled at him.

"What are you doing?" she asked.

And it was there in her eyes and in her voice. That vulnerability that made him want to tell her to protect herself. To never allow him or any other man to see how easily her barriers could be swept aside. But saying that would—what?

Would it be crueler to pretend to be a gentleman as he usually did or to just show her the bastard he really was? Because despite his royal pedigree and his much lauded charm, he was at heart a man who lived for his own pleasure.

"Proving that I don't have to use brute force to keep you by my side."

"Oh, was that what you were doing?" she asked, a smile flirting around her lips.

"Mmm hmm. What did you think it was?"

"I thought it was an act to distract Juan."

He inhaled sharply. "I'm not following."

"Yes, you are," she said, neatly stepping away from him. "You just didn't think that I'd figure out what this attention of yours was all about."

"It's about attraction, of course. You are *muy hermoso*."

She tipped her head to the side. "But that's not why you danced with me earlier or kissed me now."

He didn't like that she thought she knew what made him tick. "Why do you believe I did those things?"

"To make another woman jealous."

He started to speak but she shook her head.

"I'm not sure I want to be used, especially when you are not being up front about it."

"I apologize."

"You helped me out earlier. I suppose it's the least I can do for you now."

"What is?"

"Well, making that woman jealous...though to be honest, you probably should have picked someone more on par with her. She really is a world-class beauty."

Kara knew she'd been right about why Gui had come on to her. Despite the fact that the man could make her forget her name when he kissed her, she was determined not to be stupid where he was concerned.

"Kara." He said her name in that smooth Spanish accent of his and she wanted to pretend that whatever he said was the truth. But men like Guillermo de Cuaron didn't fall instantly for women like her.

"*Si*, Gui?"

"You do yourself a disservice," he said.

She tried to smile, but her face felt too tight and she knew she had to look like she was faking it. Which she totally was. "Well, you did it first. I'm just following you."

He cursed under his breath. "We need to talk. Somewhere that we won't be interrupted or over-heard."

"Yes, I think we do. But there is a reception going on and, as you pointed out, you are one of the groom's best friends. We should get back."

She had learned at an early age that if she took command of a situation, people would automatically follow her. There was something about a forceful tone of voice that made even the most determined man back down. She smiled as winningly as she could and decided that she wasn't going to attend any more weddings.

This had to be the worst one yet, and she was tired of torturing herself by going. No one would remark if she started skipping them. Rina always attended; she could represent their family and Kara could stay away.

"I'm not a lapdog."

"I never thought you were."

"Then stop trying to lead me around," she said.

"I don't understand you."

He shook his head and she caught a glimpse of something in his eyes. Maybe he didn't understand himself, either, but she was tired of guessing what was in his head. "Just tell me what's really going on."

He arched one eyebrow and glanced up and down the hallway. "Now?"

Kara followed his gaze. A few groups of people were drifting nearer, perhaps looking for the restroom or a little privacy. She refused to feel silly. "If it's okay to announce I'm your fiancée in the middle of the dance floor I think this hallway is okay for a serious chat."

"You're engaged, Gui?" Christos said, appearing suddenly behind Gui. How had she missed his approach?

Kara bit her lip and wanted to stomp her foot. Every time she tried to throw that bit back at him, someone overheard her. She needed to stop mentioning their "engagement" before the entire world thought it was the truth.

To Gui's credit, he wrapped an arm around her shoulder and turned so that she was tucked up next to his side. She tried not to let the way he felt pressed against her go to her head, tried not to acknowledge even to herself that there was a rightness to the way her shoulder nestled under his arm. To the way his hand felt on her back and his body heat warmed her.

"That's what we were discussing. Do you know Kara deMontaine?"

Christos nodded toward her. "Yes, I've had the pleasure of meeting Kara. Two years ago, wasn't it? At Rina's thirty-fifth?"

"Yes. Rina said that she wanted the world to know she wasn't afraid of aging."

"No one should be afraid," Christos said. "Especially a woman as beautiful as your sister."

Kara flinched and knew that Gui felt it, because he glanced down at her. She smiled, but it was forced. She hated comments like that one. Comments that inevitably made her compare herself to Rina and come up lacking.

How could she do anything but?

"I'm out here because of another beautiful woman. Sheri is looking for us—it is time for you and me to toast our best friend and his bride. So we are all needed inside."

"Of course. I better go find my friends. I'll talk to you later, Gui."

"I'll escort you," he said, refusing to let her leave his side.

As soon as they were alone she was going to talk to him about that. She had the impression that he liked to always be in control of everyone around him.

"Why thank you, I'm not sure I could walk all the way back to the reception on my own," she muttered under her breath.

Christos chuckled and shook his head as he walked away. He called back to Gui. "I'll meet you at the bridal party table."

Gui cupped her elbow and started walking back to the ballroom where the reception was being held. "Gentlemanly behavior shouldn't elicit sarcasm."

"Bossy behavior is a different story."

"I'm hardly bossy."

"You're hardly ever *not* bossy. Ever since we met you've been telling me what to do and what to think."

"Never what to think, Kara. You are too smart to let a man do that."

She smiled up at him. "Yes, I am."

He shook his head. "You're very stubborn."

"So are you. And you're arrogant to boot. Don't think I haven't noticed."

His finger rubbed against her inner arm where he held her. "I'd be disappointed if you didn't notice."

"Maybe that's why you had to resort to what you did to get a woman to be your—" She stopped talking and glanced around to make sure that there was no one close by. Just to be safe she stood on tiptoe, bracing her hands against his broad shoulders and spoke it in his ear.

"—fiancée."

He wrapped his arm around her waist and pulled her off balance so that she was supported by his body.

"I didn't resort to anything devious to get you."

Before she could think of a response, he kissed her, and even though she knew she should stop letting him end conversations by embracing her, she couldn't. No man kissed the way Gui did. Or at least no man had kissed *her* the way he did. And he made her feel the opposite of what Christos had earlier. He made her feel like she truly was a beautiful woman.

As soon as Kara reentered the ballroom, Courtney grabbed her hand. And she'd never been so glad to see her friend as she was in that moment.

"Pardon me, Count de Cuaron, but I need a word with Kara."

Gui gave Kara a kiss and then let his hand drop

away. But she wasn't sure he was going to walk away until he said, "I will see you shortly."

He bowed to Courtney before turning on his heel and striding away from them, disappearing into the well-shod crowd celebrating Tristan and Sheri's wedding.

As soon as he was out of earshot Courtney said, "What is that all about? I didn't think you even knew him."

"Of course I know him. I said I did," Kara said, regretting it more than ever.

"Yes, but you also said that you knew David Beckham."

"Well, Rina does know him, and I met him once."

"You're not Rina."

"No, I'm not," she said, aware that she was letting the conversation go into that crazy land where she'd not have to talk about Gui.

Her lips still tingled and she didn't want to dwell too much on the fact that, when he'd held her the last time, she hadn't wanted him to let go.

"So what's up with you and the Count? Emily heard someone talking in the bathroom about an engagement."

"Oh my God." She was going to be utterly humiliated if everyone was talking. There wasn't going to be a graceful way for her to back out of the "engagement." And no matter what the truth was, if the engagement ended, everyone would think Gui hadn't wanted her.

"What? Is it *true?*" Courtney asked, and for once Kara had no answers.

Kara shook her head, unwilling to lie to her friend, but the truth…she really had no idea what it was at this moment. "I have no idea."

"Um…Kara, dear, you really should know if you have a fiancé."

"It's complicated." God, she had no idea how she was going to explain this. If she told her best friends that she wasn't engaged and Gui had used her to make another woman jealous, they'd go after him. And if she said she *was* engaged… Heck, she wasn't going to say that.

"Explain *complicated,*" Courtney said.

"He and I may or may not be engaged. We're going to discuss it later."

"Holy hell."

"Courtney!"

"I think even Sister Rita Lynn would forgive me this once."

"What would Sister Rita Lynn forgive?" Katie asked as she and Emily joined them.

"My saying holy hell. Kara here may or may not be engaged to the Count."

"Don't call him that," Katie said with a little laugh. "All I can think of is the count from *Sesame Street.*"

"That sexy man reminds you of the Count?" Courtney asked.

"Enough, you two," Emily said. "We need to focus on Kara and her fiancé. When did this happen?"

Kara shook her head. This was the part that was going to sound really strange to her friends. "Today."

"The engagement happened today?" Courtney said. "Wow, I guess you really do know him."

"Gui is impetuous," Kara said, having absolutely no idea if that was usually true or not.

"Well if that's the case then it's only you that brings out that side of him," Katie said.

"What do you know about him?"

She glanced around the ballroom then leaned in close to Kara. "See that woman over there—the beautiful one in the center of that group of men?"

"Yes," Kara said. Elvira. The one who'd shaken Gui and called him *querido.* "Who is she?"

Katie glanced at Kara, and there was something in her gaze that warned Kara she might regret asking. "That's the woman he's rumored to have loved and lost. Elvira de Castillo y Perez… She's married to Count Juan de Cuaron y Perez."

"De Cuaron? Is he related to Gui?" Kara asked.

"They're cousins by marriage," Katie said. "Juan is related to the Enfanta of Spain—Gui's sister-in-law."

"So what does that woman have to do with Kara?" Emily asked.

"Yeah, so what if he loved her and lost her? Clearly that's ancient history, right?" Courtney asked.

"It happened over ten years ago. Apparently Elvira tried to use jealousy to force Gui to marry her and he refused, so she married Juan."

"Well, then there's nothing to worry about there," Kara said.

"I wouldn't say so. Rumors are all over the Spanish Court and practically every court in Europe about Elvira and Gui. Seems marriage didn't stop them from continuing their affair," Katie said.

Katie worked for a European news network and was the host of a nightly celebrity show similar to the *Ten Spot* on E! She always knew the best gossip and usually was able to tell the truth from the rumors.

"Really?" Kara asked.

"That's the rumor. The thing is, aside from Juan's jealousy, no one else can substantiate anything about the alleged affair. His friends all say that Gui respects the bonds of marriage."

"That's something," Courtney said.

"Yes, it is," Kara agreed. But a part of her wondered if respecting the bonds of marriage was enough to keep Gui from the woman he'd loved and lost. Because she'd sensed there was more to him and Elvira than simply old friends when they'd talked on the dance floor.

She turned with the crowd to watch Gui at the mike, offering the wedding toast along with Christos, charming the crowd. He was eloquent and a tad romantic without being patronizing. The kind of man she'd dreamed of finding.

She glanced around the ballroom and knew the gap between her and Gui was literal. He fit here in their social world the way she never had. And now that she knew more of his past, she wondered what exactly he thought pretending to be engaged to her was going to accomplish. Because Kara knew one thing with absolute certainty—she wasn't the type of woman who'd make Elvira jealous.

Four

"A wedding night... I never thought I'd have one again," Tristan said as he paced around the living room of the hotel suite. Sheri was in the other suite with her bridesmaids, getting changed into a fashionable outfit for leaving the reception.

"Wedding nights are the only reason I'd consider marriage," Gui said.

"With Kara deMontaine?" Christos asked.

"With any woman," he said, not ready to discuss anything involving Kara with his friends.

"Rumor has it you're engaged," Tristan said.

"How the hell did *you* hear a rumor? You were

supposed to be completely enthralled with your beautiful bride."

"I was. Blame my sister. Blanche is good friends with Rina deMontaine…"

"Those women are faster than CNN at spreading news," Gui muttered. He crossed the room to the wet bar and poured himself two fingers of Scotch. He swallowed the drink quickly.

"So is it true?" Christos asked, coming up next to him.

"Yes," Gui said. He would have to convince Kara that engagement was next for them, and God knew how he'd do it. But there was no way he was going to tell his friends that in a moment of weakness he'd claimed her as his own.

"What about Elvira?" Tristan asked.

"Last time I checked, Tris, she was married."

"You know what I mean."

Gui scrubbed a hand over his face. "It's past time for me to move on."

"I agree. Kara's a good choice for you."

"She is?" Gui asked. He knew nothing about the woman except that she had the softest lips he'd ever tasted and when he kissed her he forgot that all other women existed.

Not a bad start to an affair, but marriage… Damn, was he really considering marrying her? With Tristan's words echoing in his mind, he knew that he was indeed considering it. It made sense to him.

His friends were all married now, and he wanted the dynamic between the three of them to stay the same. If he were the only bachelor, there would be things he couldn't participate in with them. Couple things. The very things Gui had spent his entire adult life avoiding.

But now…now those things seemed appealing for some reason, and Kara deMontaine…well, she was someone he could easily see by his side.

"What do you know of her?"

"She's active with several women and children's groups. All of her charitable work is focused on family," Tristan said, pouring a glass of Scotch for himself and taking a sip.

"She'd make a good addition to the Cuaron Foundation," Gui said. He'd started the Cuaron Foundation nearly ten years ago to help keep kids off drugs through getting them outside and active in extreme sports. The foundation was based in Madrid, and most of the work he did was in Europe, but he had started a second location in Australia last year. And he'd always planned to bring the foundation to the United States.

"She would," Christos said. "I remember when I

talked to her at Rina's birthday party last year that she was intelligent and very well-spoken if a bit shy."

Gui knew the root of that shyness. And wasn't surprised that she'd overcome it to talk to Christos. She was too bold a spirit to let anything hold her back when she was passionate about something. And she must be about her work.

"When is the wedding to take place?" Tristan asked.

Gui poured himself more Scotch. He wasn't even sure he could convince Kara to marry him. And he knew that she wouldn't just agree because of who he was, as a number of other women would. That knowledge only made her more appealing. He realized that, for the first time since he had met Elvira, another woman and her passion were consuming him.

He was concerned, because passion like that burned bright and fast and usually left burn marks to match. Gui had learned a lot in the last ten years of being relegated to the sidelines of the life of a woman he'd wanted so passionately.

What exactly had he learned? he wondered.

"We haven't picked a date. I don't know that it's going to be a big ceremony," Gui said.

"Are you kidding?" Christos said, reaching around to pour himself a drink before going back to the couch and sitting down. "Rina's not going to let her baby sister get married in a quickie ceremony. And I doubt your mother would be too pleased if you didn't give her a proper ceremony to attend."

Christos had a good point. This was getting too damned complicated. If he was going to control Kara and the situation the way he wanted to, he was going to have to sweep her off her feet and have a whirlwind courtship and marriage.

Marriage, he thought again. To Kara deMontaine? He'd thought to never give his name to a woman. But he knew he'd have to produce an heir, because his older brother's offspring were heirs to the royal throne and it fell to Gui to produce heirs for his family.

"We're not going to let my mother or Rina decide anything about our wedding," Gui said.

Christos choked on his drink. "Women look at these things differently, Gui."

"Some women might, but Kara isn't like that. She's in love with me and will follow my direction on this," he said.

"Every woman in love dreams of a big wedding to her man," Tristan said. "I have a sister, I know this…you should, too."

"Some situations are more delicate and require a quicker timeline."

Christos put his glass on the coffee table and stood up. "Are you saying she's with child?"

"No, she's not with child. She's in love and has insisted we get married as quickly as possible." Gui started to lift the Scotch glass to his mouth but put it down. He needed to stop drinking and start thinking things through.

Kara was tired by the time the bride and groom left. She'd been careful to keep her distance from Gui when he'd returned to the reception area. He was with the bridal party, so it was easy to keep track of him.

For one brief moment, as she watched him standing to the side of the other couples in the party, she felt a pang. He looked so distant and alone. And a part of her recognized that loneliness, because she'd experienced the same thing many times.

Heck, that was the reason he'd singled her out earlier today.

"Ms. deMontaine?" The man who spoke to her was shorter than she was and at least fifty years old. He was dressed in a very fashionable suit and tie, all black and white, and she could tell just from the way he carried himself that he probably worked for one of the families in attendance here.

"Yes?"

"I am Vincent Montez," he said with a slight bow. "Count de Cuaron has asked that you meet him upstairs."

She smiled at the older man. "Please give the Count my regrets."

He nodded and bowed once more before leaving her. Kara knew that her time to get gone was shortening. This situation, which had never really been in her control, was close to getting completely out of it.

She had ridden to the ceremony with Courtney but, when she glanced over at her friend, she noticed that the redhead was in an intimate conversation with a man. Kara took out her cell phone and sent a quick text message to Courtney, telling her she'd call in the morning, and made her way out of the ballroom.

She'd have a good night's sleep and then worry about her rumored engagement in the morning. She'd been amazed at how quickly gossip had spread at the reception. Everyone was talking about her and Gui, and Kara wasn't in the mood to keep her happy smile in place for another second.

She would hail a cab and go home and then break the box of special dishes that she kept on hand for exercising her temper. Because she didn't believe in wasting anything, she only broke plates that the kids at the shelter could use to make mosaic birdbaths.

"Kara."

"Damn."

"Damn? You don't strike me as a woman who curses."

"Count Guillermo, tonight I am."

He chuckled. "Long one?"

"Yes. Funny how a rumored engagement to a very eligible bachelor can do that to a girl."

"May I give you a lift home?"

"Do you have a car?"

"Indeed."

"That'd be lovely. I was going to take a cab."

"Then allow me."

"I will. It's the least you can do for your *fiancée*."

"If my *fiancée* wasn't so stubborn—"

"I'm not stubborn. I just know my mind."

"Stubborn," he said under his breath.

"The same could be said of you."

"To be honest, it has been," he said.

She almost smiled at him, because this was the first moment when she saw him as more than a sexy man. She saw the real man beneath the aristocratic title and charm.

"Where's your car?"

"I sent Vincent to get it."

She nodded. "I guess he delivered my message."

"Yes, he did. Why wouldn't you come upstairs to see me?"

"Because I'm American and I prefer to be asked by the man who wants to see me and not his servant."

"Vincent is more than a servant. He's a friend and trusted advisor."

"My mistake."

"How could you ever doubt your appeal to the opposite sex?" he asked.

"Easily," she said. "I'm usually very shy around men. But somehow, knowing you are my…whatever, has loosened my tongue. Either that, or all the martinis I had earlier. I wonder if I've had too much to drink?"

"You haven't."

"How do you know?" she asked. She doubted he'd been paying much attention to her all night long.

"A man likes to think he knows his own fiancée."

"Yeah, but I'm not really—"

"Not really what?"

Kara heard the haughty feminine voice with that sexy Spanish accent and knew that Countess Elvira was there behind them. She put her hand on Gui's forearm and glanced back at the other woman.

She wanted to tell the woman to mind her own business. And Kara was sure she saw something in the other woman's eyes that indicated she knew the truth. Somehow Elvira knew that she and Gui weren't really engaged.

"I'm not really tired," Kara said at last.

Gui wrapped an arm around her waist and drew her back against his body, dropping a kiss along the side of her neck. "We'll think of something to do when we get back to your place."

Any other woman would have looked away, but not Elvira. Kara knew, because she saw the flush of anger in the other woman when she opened her own eyes.

"Gui is an excellent lover, isn't he?"

Kara felt the blush that climbed up her neck and face. She traveled on the very outer edges of this sophisticated crowd, but she wasn't jaded. She never had been.

"Leave her alone, Elvira."

"*Querido,* have your tastes changed so drastically?"

"Not at all," he said.

"Then how can you be with…"

"She's the woman I've been waiting for, Elvira. A woman worth marrying."

Gui led her away from the other woman and out the front door where Vincent had a Rolls-Royce waiting for them. They climbed in the backseat without saying a word, but Kara's mind was busy with the thought that there were worse pains than embarrassment, and if she didn't watch herself around Gui, she might end up with a broken heart.

* * *

The apartment that Gui kept in Manhattan was on Park Avenue and overlooked Central Park. He'd had it for years and had always thought that he had the best there was in the city, but Kara's place was lovely. There was something very fresh and American about her decor and the feeling he got when he stepped over the threshold.

She put her handbag on a table in the foyer before leading the way into a well-appointed den. There were floor-to-ceiling bookcases along three walls, and three overstuffed chairs and a large leather couch grouped together in front of a large walnut desk. The executive chair behind it was leather, to match the sofa. The desk had a laptop on it and two picture frames. He wondered whose photos she kept on her desk.

"Have a seat, Gui."

She walked around behind the desk and sat down. He bit the inside of his lip at her play for power.

Instead of sitting, he leaned one hip on the edge of her desk. Her den was one of the most relaxing rooms he'd ever been in. And he realized that there was something about Kara that brought a sense of peace to him.

Peace was something he rarely experienced. "Where should we start this discussion of ours?"

"I think at the beginning. Why did you say I was your fiancée?"

Gui pushed to his feet and paced around the room. He really had no explanation. He knew only that he had needed to change the dynamic between himself and Elvira. He hadn't thought of the impact on Kara.

He stopped in front of a floor-to-ceiling window that looked out to the east. The lights of the city spread out before him. It was a view he was used to—remote. He often felt a bit removed from life, except when he was working with the kids through his foundation. He even kept a distance from his lovers.

"Gui? Is it true that she was the one woman you loved?" She'd given up her seat behind the desk to stand near him at the window.

"Where did you hear that?"

"From Katie. She works for the Celebrity Channel."

He shook his head. "Don't listen to gossip, Kara."

"I don't. That's why I'm asking you. What's between you and Elvira?"

"Ancient history."

"Is it true you and she are lovers?"

"Kara, I said leave it be."

"I can't *leave it be,* Gui. She's the reason you said we were engaged, and now my family and friends want to know if I'm going to marry you. And I have no idea what to say to them."

"What do you want to say?"

She nibbled on her lower lip, reaching out to touch the glass. "A part of me wants to say yes, I am going to marry you. Which is silly, because I don't know you. But I'm at the age where people— Okay, *I'm* starting to wonder if I'm ever going to be married."

He turned to her then, knowing there was no backing down. Though he'd have done it if Kara had seemed to have more doubts.

"I never planned to marry," he said, feeling the need to be totally honest. "I'm not sure that I'm husband material, but my life is at a point…"

"I understand. Mine is, too. If we went through with this, I'd want to set up some criteria for our relationship."

"Why?"

"Because I could easily fool myself into falling for you, Count, and I'm not really into heartbreak."

"Neither am I. I don't want to hurt you, Kara. But love isn't something that I believe in."

"But you have such a close-knit family, surely you love them?"

"I have great affection for my sisters and for my brother and parents. But that's not the kind of love you're talking about."

"No, it isn't. I mean romantic love. What did you feel for Elvira?"

"Passion," he said, feeling he owed her some

kind of explanation. "Jealousy and obsession. It was a volatile relationship. And I'm not interested in experiencing that again."

"Well, I've never stirred a man's passionate nature," she said. And he heard in her voice that hint of longing. He stared into her eyes, just inches below his. *Sexy.* "Gui?"

"Stop saying things like that. You stir passion very easily in me. It's just not fueled by the darker emotions."

"You stir me, too, Gui. That's another reason why I'm contemplating this. I've never really been attracted to another man."

"You are a virgin?" he asked, a part of him pleased to think of being the first man to have Kara.

She shook her head. "No, I'm not."

He shook off the twinge of jealousy he felt toward her unnamed past lovers. He knew it was irrational. He'd had many lovers, but he wanted her to be as innocent as she looked.

"You aren't either, right?"

He bit the inside of his lip to keep from smiling at the way she said that. "No, I'm not. I was simply inquiring because you said you hadn't been attracted to another man."

"Well, sex can be about something other than passion," she said.

"No, it can't. Passion is the only reason a man and a woman should share their bodies."

"And you think we have passion between us?" she asked.

"I know we do," he said, lowering his head to capture her lips and prove to her that passion was the one thing they could both agree they had between them.

Five

Kara had spent most of her life feeling alone and lost in the sea of people around her. But in Gui's arms she felt anchored for the first time since her mother had died.

Rina had always tried to give her an inner strength and was the best big sister anyone could have, but Kara's self-doubts were rooted in her own body image. But in Gui's arms she didn't feel too big or too fat. His kisses and caresses left no room for doubts.

His mouth moved over hers, igniting a fire inside her body that she'd never experienced before. This was the kind of lust that she heard others talk about. Was it this way for Gui all the time? With every woman he took in his arms?

She knew better than to ask. She closed her eyes and wrapped her arms around his shoulders as he angled his head for a deeper kiss. His lips were firm and sure as he moved his mouth over hers then dropped nibbling kisses along the line of her jaw and down her neck.

She shivered.

"Do you like that, *mi dulce?*"

"Hmm mmm."

"Kara?"

She opened her eyes, meeting his hazel gaze. He hugged her close to him and she felt his erection nudge her lower stomach. She swallowed and tried to stop from rubbing herself against him but she couldn't help it.

"Do you want me?" he asked, his voice low and sexy with that Spanish accent.

"Yes, Gui. I do."

"I want you, too, *bebe.*"

He leaned down again and this time bit her neck softly. His hands skimmed over her sides and he drew her up into his body. With her heels on she didn't have to stretch too much to meet his lips when they came down on hers again.

She felt the impact of his lips on hers all the way down her body. Her breasts felt fuller and her nipples tightened in the lacy bra cups she wore under her haute couture dress. She shifted against him, moving one leg apart from the other one and wrapping it around his leg.

She needed to get closer to him. She wanted to feel his hot, hard erection pressed to her center. She was moist and ready for him and all he'd done was kiss her.

They were both still fully clothed and she was going crazy in his arms. It was as if she were another person. She was both aroused and scared. The feelings Gui was evoking in her were foreign… addictive.

She felt his hands slide up her back, rubbing in a circular motion until he reached the back of her head. He tangled his fingers in her hair, spilling the pins that held her hair up in its fancy do. He took hold of her head and leaned her back so that she was arched in his arms.

His mouth moved from hers again, this time biting and kissing her neck. With his free hand, he found the zipper hidden in the side of her bodice and lowered it.

The dress gaped away from her body and Gui tugged on the fabric until he revealed her breasts. She glanced down at herself, clothing askew and her bra-covered breasts straining. She was breathing heavily.

She wanted more of Gui. He was breathing deeply, his face flushed with arousal. He traced the edge of the lacy cup of her bra. She quivered under his touch, reaching out to grasp his shoulders to ground herself in this moment.

He slipped a finger under the fabric and traced her nipple. She shivered again and felt too exposed as he stared down at her. All of her body-image issues came to the surface. Especially when he reached around her body to undo the back clasp of her bra.

He loosened the fabric and began to draw it away from her breasts, but she brought her hand up to stop him. "I'm not slim like the women you're used to seeing."

Gui lifted her in his arms, something no man had ever done, and carried her to the leather sofa. He sat down and arranged her on his lap.

"Kara, *mi dulce,* you are exactly as you should be. I'm not thinking of any woman but you."

She was ruining the moment. She should keep her mouth shut, but she'd die—absolutely die—if he managed to take her clothes off and then was repulsed by her soft body. "I'm just trying to let you know that I look better with my clothes on."

"I'm not doing a proper job of arousing you if you are worried about what you look like naked. You should be enjoying the feelings I'm evoking in you."

She smiled up at him, lifting herself to kiss him. It was a gentle kiss. "I have never enjoyed myself more, Gui."

He waggled his eyebrows at her. "Good."

He lowered his head to hers again and kissed her slowly, and she thought about the lights that she'd turned on when they'd entered the room. If she could just get up and turn them off…

Gui lifted his mouth from hers and a second later she felt the warmth of his tongue on her nipple. She arched on his lap as his lips closed over it and he began to suckle her.

A restless need swept through her and she clutched his head to her breast as her legs scissored apart. She was on fire for him. Each pull of his mouth on her breast caused a chain reaction in her body.

Gui's other hand slid up her leg and she reveled in the feel of his big warm hand against her. Then his fingers slipped downward toward her center.

He traced her shape through the fabric of her panties, ran his forefinger down the center of her. She shifted her legs and arched against his hand.

Then he moved her panties to the side and she felt the touch of his finger against her intimate flesh. She was quivering on the edge of an orgasm. And when his finger moved over her exposed flesh in the same rhythm as his mouth against her nipple, she knew she wasn't going to last long.

She still held his head to her breast and her hips lifted up toward his hand. She felt one finger dip into the wetness inside her body. She arched into his touch, needing more of him, and his name fell from her lips as he continued to caress her. He lifted his head from her breast, blew gently on her nipple before looking at her.

"Come for me, Kara," he said.

She shivered at the intimate command, and then he thrust two fingers deep inside her while his thumb pressed down, and she shook in his arms, her orgasm startling her. She grabbed his shoulders as he continued to hold her through the climax. She called his name and turned her face into his chest so he wouldn't be able to see her when she felt that vulnerable.

She stayed there, wrapped in his arms, trying to remember that they weren't the romantic love match of the year. No matter how perfect he felt to her at this moment or how much she might secretly want them to be.

Gui was hard and wanted nothing more than to bury himself in the humid warmth of Kara, to feel her long limbs wrapped around his hips as he drove into her. But there was a sweet vulnerability to this woman and he sensed that if he pushed too hard now, he'd lose her.

And somewhere between his careless comments to Elvira and now, he'd realized that he didn't want to lose her. She was the solution that he'd been searching for.

"Thank you, Gui."

"For what, *bebe?*"

"For that," she said, blushing. His hand was still between her legs, her breast still bared to his gaze, and she was blushing over a word. He knew she didn't feel uncomfortable at this moment, because if she did she would cover herself.

Her thighs were soft and smooth and a nice pale color that contrasted with his own olive skin tone. He leaned down to kiss her.

"You're very welcome."

She shifted on his lap against his erection. "Um…you're not finished, are you?"

"Finished with what, *querida?*"

"Making love with me," she said softly. She lifted her hand and cupped his jaw. Her fingers were long and cool against his skin and he felt charmed by the way she touched him. The way she looked at him. She made him feel as if he were the only man on earth. And more of a hero than he'd ever felt before.

"For now," he said.

She tried to sit up and draw her dress over her body at the same time, upsetting her balance, and she fell off his lap. He grabbed her arm, holding her in place.

"Stop. I'll help you."

"That's okay," she said, her voice small and tight and her expression so closed that he knew he'd done something to hurt her.

But he had no idea what. He was being a gentleman here. Did she honestly think he didn't want to be buried inside her silky body right this instant?

He took her wrists in his hands and held them in her lap. She was shaking and he didn't think it was with rage. "What is going on?"

"I just want to get dressed so we can get back to our discussion."

"But you were content to lie here a minute ago."

"Please, Gui. I need to get up."

"Why?" he asked.

She jerked hard on her wrists. And he held her fast, careful not to hurt her. "I want some answers, Kara. Please."

She bit her lower lip and he thought he saw that sheen of tears in her eyes again. He definitely saw that sadness that had been on her face at the cathedral earlier.

"What is it, *bebe?* I am trying to respect you, not push too hard. Why does that make you sad?"

"Is it really about respect?" she asked, then lowered her head so he couldn't see her pretty eyes.

He cupped the back of her neck and drew her toward him, let her rest her face against his shoulder. "Of course it is. Why else would I stop now?"

"Maybe you were looking at my body and saw how flabby I am… Maybe that made you not want me."

He shook his head. "You aren't flabby, Kara. Trust me on this."

"I'm a size twelve. You may not know what that size is, but it's big. Large. I'm a large girl, Gui."

He shook his head again and took one of her hands in his, drew it down between both of their bodies until it rested on the outline of his erection where it strained against the zipper of his dress pants.

"Does that really feel like a man who doesn't want you?"

She caressed him through his pants and shifted on his lap so that she straddled his hips. The fabric of the dress fell over his hips and their hands. Her fingers traced the length of him, and she reached for the tab of his zipper. Before he could stop her, she drew it down.

He felt her fingers on his naked flesh and groaned

deep in his throat, realizing that all his noble thoughts of stopping, of keeping this moment pure for her, were fading quickly.

He wanted her and she wasn't saying no. So why should he deny them both what they wanted? He needed her. He didn't question why. Kara had drawn him from the first moment he'd seen her.

She wrapped her hand around him, sliding up and down his length. When she drew her hand down she reached to lower his pants. But the fabric was still too tight the way they were sitting.

He sat up. "Kiss me while I take care of this."

She cupped his face in both of her hands. Her lips brushed his, a simple back and forth motion that made him twitch. Then she caught his lower lip between her teeth and bit down gently, sucking him into her mouth.

He lifted his hips and shoved his pants down until he was completely free of them. Then he reached under her skirt and drew her panties down her legs. She continued to kiss him but shifted her legs so that he could remove her underwear.

Then she lifted her head and straddled him again. He put his hands on her waist and drew her down until they were pressed against each other.

"Are you sure, Gui?"

"Incredibly sure," he said, realizing he wasn't

just talking about making love to her. He was also one hundred percent positive that he'd found the woman that he would marry.

"I guess you are turned on." Her hand brushed over his straining length again.

"Hell, yes," he said, pulling her to him. He lifted her slightly so that he could remove her dress. He drew it up over her body and tossed it aside, then he pulled her bra off and held her naked in his arms.

She crossed her arms over her chest and pressed into him, he was sure to cover her nakedness. "I want to see you."

"No, you don't," she said. She leaned back just enough to loosen his tie and toss it aside. Then she went to work on the buttons of his dress shirt, and he helped her remove both it and his jacket. Once he was bare chested he took her wrists in his hands and drew them behind her back so that he could look at her body.

She was soft, her skin white as alabaster and supple. There was a slight bump where her tummy was and her full breasts rested against her rib cage. She was turning red from the curves of her breasts up to her neck.

"Why are you embarrassed?" he asked.

She tugged on her hands. "Why do you always hold on to my hands?"

"So that I can keep you where I want you."

"That's not a very attractive thing to do."

"You're too independent. Earlier you tried to leave me, and now you are trying to hide from me."

She nodded at him. "I'm trying to hide because I know that I won't match up with the other women you've taken to your bed. And all this talk of being your fiancée has made me consider really going through with it, so I don't want you to change your mind."

"Kara, *bebe,* I'd never change my mind because of this. You are incredibly lovely and turn me on like no other woman has."

"Gui…please don't lie to me. It's okay to say you want me, and for us to have sex—"

He kissed her to quiet her down. He didn't want to hear anything else she had to say right now. Words weren't going to convince Kara that she was the woman he wanted. In fact, he was positive the only thing that would convince her was action.

He drew her forward. She bit on her lip as his chest brushed against her nipples.

"I like that," she said.

Blood roared in his ears. He was so hard, so full right now that he needed to be inside of her body. He caressed her creamy thighs. God, she was soft. She moaned as he neared her center and then sighed when he brushed his fingertips across her. He slipped one finger into her body. She was warm and wet and her muscles tightened around his finger. He hesitated for a second, looking into her eyes.

Her eyelids were half-closed. She bit down on her lower lip and he felt the minute movements of her hips as she tried to move his touch where she needed it.

He pulled her head down to his so he could taste her. Her mouth opened over his and he told himself to take it slow, but slow wasn't in his programming with this woman. She was pure feminine temptation and he had her in his arms.

He nibbled on her and held her at his mercy. Her nails dug into his shoulders as he caressed her spine, feathering his fingers down the length of her back to the indentation above her backside.

She closed her eyes and held her breath as he moved one hand around to run a finger over her nipple. It was velvety compared to the satin smoothness of her breast. He brushed his finger back and forth until she shifted on his lap. He wanted to give her so much pleasure, because he felt it was a man's job to make the woman he was with confident in her sexuality. And Kara was one woman who should definitely feel confident.

Seeing the sexy, confident woman she was disappear when she talked about her body had made him angry. Women were vulnerable when it came to sex. Not in just a physical way, but in an emotional one as well, and Gui made it a point to make sure that his lovers knew how sexy and beautiful he found them.

She moaned, a sweet sound that he leaned up to capture with his mouth. She tipped her head to the side immediately allowing him greater access.

She shivered in his arms. He pushed her back a little bit so he could see her. Her breasts were bare, nipples distended and begging for his mouth. He lowered his head and suckled.

He held one hand on the small of her back and buried his other in her hair. He had a lap full of woman and he knew that he wanted Kara more than he'd wanted any other woman in a long time.

Her eyes were closed, her hips moving subtly against him, and when he blew on her nipple he saw gooseflesh spread down her body. He bit carefully at the lily-white skin of her chest, suckling at her so that he'd leave his mark. He wanted her to remember this moment and what they had done when she was alone later.

She rocked her hips harder against his length and he thrust against her. He bit down gently on her tender, aroused nipple. She cried his name and he hurriedly covered her mouth with his, wanting to feel every bit of her passion.

He rocked her until the storm passed and she quieted in his arms. He was so hard he thought he'd die if he didn't get inside her.

He glanced at her and saw that she was watching him. The fire in her eyes made his entire body tight with anticipation.

Only an idiot would have unprotected sex without asking a woman about her sexual history. But that could break the mood so he just reached for the condom he'd put in his pocket before the wedding, knowing he wouldn't want to be alone tonight. He put the condom on one-handed and said, "I really want you. Come to me now."

Shifting on his lap, she invited him into her body. He put his hands on her waist and held her still, wanting this moment when he first took her to last forever.

He needed to be inside her now. Using his hands on her waist he held her still and then shifted his legs so he could thrust up into her.

"Ready to take me, *bebe?*"

"Yes, Gui."

"Look at me this first time. Let me see your eyes as I make you mine."

Her hands fluttered between them and their eyes met.

He held her hips steady and entered her slowly,

until he was fully seated. Her eyes widened. She clutched at his arms as he started thrusting, holding him to her, eyes half-closed and her head tipped back.

He caught one of her nipples in his teeth, scraping very gently. She started to tighten around him. Her hips moved faster, demanding more, but he kept the pace slow, steady, wanting her to come before he did.

He suckled her nipple and rotated his hips to catch her pleasure point with each thrust, and he felt her hands in his hair, clenching, as she threw her head back and her climax ripped through her.

He varied his thrusts, finding a rhythm that would draw out the tension at the base of his spine. Something that would make his time in her body, wrapped in her silky limbs, last forever.

He tipped her hips up to give him deeper access to her body. Then she scraped her nails down his back. His blood roared in his ears as he felt everything in his world center to this one woman.

He called her name as he came.

Six

Kara woke in her own bed alone, to the smell of freshly brewed coffee. The automatic blinds on her window were still closed so she knew it was before nine, which was when she normally woke and started her day. As she sat up, the covers fell to her waist and she was startled at her own nudity.

Then everything rushed back to her. Gui and the night they'd spent in each other's arms.

"Good morning, *mi dulce*. Did you sleep well?"

She glanced to the sitting area to the left of the bed and found Gui on her chaise longue, a breakfast tray with coffee and scones next to him, the *New York Times* neatly folded on his lap.

She gulped. And tried to find words. She'd been so in control in her den… Ha. She hadn't been in control for a single moment since she'd met Gui.

"I slept fine," she said.

"Coffee?"

"That would be nice."

"Cream or sugar?"

"Just cream," she said, then wrapped the sheets around her body and leaned back against the headboard. The two men she'd had as lovers before Gui had never spent the night, and frankly she had absolutely no idea what to do with him this morning.

He brought her a cup of coffee with a saucer. When she reached for it, he held it just out of her reach.

"May I please have the coffee?"

He handed it to her and sat on the bed. He was so close that she worried about her morning breath. Then she worried about her hair, which often resembled Medusa's snakes first thing in the morning. Then she wondered if she had a crease in her face from the pillowcase.

She set her coffee mug down on the nightstand. "I need a minute in the…" What did they call the bathroom in Spain? In the UK it was the toilet or water closet and she was making a complete mess of this when all she wanted was for everything to be perfect.

"Of course. Where is your robe? I'll bring it to you."

"Hanging in my closet on a hook to the right, but, um…you don't have to go get it."

"Forgive me," he said with a slight bow. "I'd much rather see you naked."

She blushed. Seriously blushed. "The robe would be very nice."

He chuckled as he walked away. Last night, when he'd made love to her, she'd forgotten her body issues, but this morning they were all back. She leaned over the edge of her bed, trying to catch a glimpse of herself in the mirror over her dressing table. Her hair was as bad as she'd feared. Repeated pats wouldn't make it stay down.

"My lady," Gui said as he returned.

She stopped messing with her hair and tried to smile at him, but it had to look strained. She took the robe he held out to her and drew it on while trying to keep the covers in place.

She finally had it wrapped around her and got out of the bed. As soon as she did Gui drew her into his arms and kissed her.

She forgot about the fact that she had morning breath and Medusa hair. She wrapped her arms around his lean waist and rested against him for a moment. She knew this was an illusion, that they weren't a couple in the throes of falling in love, but for this one moment she wanted to pretend they were.

"We didn't make any decisions last night," she said when he drew back.

"Go take care of your business and then we will talk."

"I'm not sure that talking is going to help us."

"Trust me, it will. Our engagement is on Page Six of the *Post*. At this point I think we need to decide how we are going to handle it."

"Are we engaged?" she asked. She still wasn't sure after last night. He'd held her close, slept with her all through the night, waking her twice to make love to her again. Each time she'd welcomed him into her body—and, she admitted to herself, into her heart.

She'd wanted to wrap her legs and arms around him the last time and keep him there forever. Because when Gui made love to her, she forgot all the insecurities that dogged her the rest of the time.

"What are you thinking?"

"Um…nothing."

He shook his head. "Your eyes are so expressive, *bebe*. Do you know that?"

She shook her head.

"Well, they are."

"What do you think you see in my eyes?" she asked.

"Passion. Do you want me again, Kara?" he asked, drawing his finger along the edge of her robe.

She shivered under his touch. Of course she wanted him. And his touching her only brought the passion in her to the fore. She leaned toward him, going up on her tiptoes to meet his mouth as it came down toward hers.

He tasted of minty toothpaste and coffee. His tongue tangled with hers and then stroked into her mouth with long languid kisses.

His arms came around her, drawing her more securely into the curves of his body. She held on to his shoulders and knew that, whatever was happening between them, they were definitely still going to be lovers.

The bedroom door opened with a loud bang. "Kara—"

Gui took his time finishing the kiss even though Kara tried to pull free as she recognized her sister's voice.

"Good morning, Rina," Gui said. He hugged Kara close and dropped two more kisses on her mouth. "Go, *mi dulce*. I will entertain your sister until you come back."

Kara hesitated for a second, but seeing the shocked look on Rina's face made up her mind. She needed to brush her teeth and hair before she took on Rina *and* Gui. And she had a feeling she was going to need more than one cup of coffee to deal with the world this morning.

"Count de Cuaron, what are you doing in Kara's bedroom this morning?"

"I'm her fiancé, Rina. Where else would I be?"

"Don't mess with me. I'm not sure what's going on here, but if you think for one minute that I'm going to let you use Kara in the game you're playing with Elvira—"

"Kara has nothing to do with Elvira." Gui cut her off. His original announcement might have been made in reaction to Elvira's presence at Tristan's reception, but the situation no longer had anything to do with his old lover.

He'd never sleep with Kara just to prove something to Elvira. He'd seen firsthand how out of control that kind of situation could become. And he wasn't interested in seeing Kara hurt.

"It doesn't look that way to me, or to the rest of polite society."

"I don't care what the world thinks."

"Well, *I* do. Kara has spent her entire life avoiding the spotlight. She doesn't deserve to be thrust into it because of your indiscretion."

"What exactly are you objecting to? Your sister is my fiancée."

"I'm objecting to the fact that she has no ring. That I haven't heard the first word about you from my sister's lips. And finally, I'm objecting because I don't trust you, Guillermo."

Gui tamped down on his temper as he listened to Rina going on about how he needed to realize that Kara wasn't alone or vulnerable. He heard the snick of the bathroom door and turned to see Kara standing there. She was dressed in a long skirt and a slim-fitting sweater. She had her hair pulled back at the base of her neck and he noticed she'd put on makeup.

"Rina, I'm not twelve anymore. You don't have to rush to my rescue and fight my battles."

"Indeed, she doesn't. I'm here to fight them for you now," Gui said, because he wanted Rina to realize that she'd been replaced in Kara's life. Did he really want to be responsible for this woman's happiness? A quick glance at her left him confused. He wanted her. Marrying her would give him what he wanted and needed to stay a peer with his best friends. But to be honest, he'd never had to worry about anyone save himself, and he liked it that way.

"Really, Count? Because I had a very interesting

conversation this morning with Count Juan, and he assures me that you were sniffing around Elvira just last week. So when exactly did you become engaged to my sister?"

"Rina, back off. We need a minute and then we'll meet you downstairs in the breakfast room. Please ask Cynthia to prepare my usual breakfast."

Rina looked like she didn't want to leave, but Kara stood her ground and Gui found a new respect for her. She might seem to be a soft, sweet girl, but there was a core of inner strength to her.

"Fine. But I don't have all day. I'm due at the club for tennis in little over an hour."

"Understood. We'll be right down."

Rina left the room, closing the door firmly behind her. Kara crossed to her coffee cup and took a long sip. "Is there anything else I should know about you and Elvira before we go downstairs?"

"There is nothing between Elvira and me, and there hasn't been in over ten years."

"Are you pining for her?"

"No. And I've told you I won't discuss her with you."

Kara nodded. "Okay. Then I have only one more question for you."

"Go ahead."

She took another sip of her coffee and then

crossed the room to put her cup and saucer on the tray before looking at him again.

"Do you want to marry me?"

He considered it one more time, because he knew that once he committed himself to Kara, he'd have given his word, and his word was one thing he prided himself on keeping.

"Yes," he said at last. "I do want to marry you, Kara. I think we'd make a good match, and we have passion between us. There's little more that any couple can ask for."

She bit her lower lip. "What about love?"

He opened his mouth to respond, but she laughed before he could.

"That's right, you don't believe in romantic love. Well I'm a bit of a silly girl at times, Gui, and I do believe in it. So I'm going to have to ask you one more question."

"Go ahead."

"If you marry me, will you be true to our marriage vows? Because the one thing I can't stand is infidelity. If you fall in love with someone else, I'd expect you to come to me and tell me."

"What would you do if that happened?" he asked, knowing it wouldn't, because he had never felt even the slightest twinge of love for a woman. Passion, lust, fiery temper, obsession, sure, but love? Never.

"I would be upset, of course, but we'd divorce and I'd give you leave to pursue the woman you loved," she said at last.

He nodded, understanding what she was asking him. He'd never been in a monogamous relationship before, and he had no idea how long it would appeal to him. But his brother had made a success of his marriage, as had his father and uncles. There was no reason why he couldn't, as well.

"If I fall in love with someone else, I'll expect you to do the same."

He shook his head. "No. You will not fall in love with anyone else."

"Gui—"

"This isn't open for negotiation, Kara. You will not look at another man or flirt with another man. Once you have committed yourself to me, you will be true to that bond."

"Yet there is a chance you might not be?" she asked, crossing her arms over her chest.

"Highly doubtful, *mi dulce*. But I've never contented myself with only one woman before…"

"Gui, you're not doing a good job of convincing me to marry you."

"I believe you already have decided to, and we are just ironing out the details now."

* * *

Two days later Kara still wasn't sure how she'd come to agree to marry Guillermo. He'd taken complete control of planning their wedding. She'd been wined and dined all over Manhattan, and now she was on an evening flight on his private jet to Madrid. He insisted there was only one place in the world where he could get his favorite breakfast.

Vincent, Gui's secretary/butler, was accompanying them, as was Cynthia, Kara's assistant, who always traveled with her. Gui was busy at his desk on one side of the plane, answering e-mails and talking on the phone.

Kara tried to relax but she couldn't. All of her friends thought that Gui was the most romantic man they'd ever met, and to some extent Kara agreed with them, because she was the one basking in his attention. But there was another part of her that knew he was acting like a loving man to spin the gossip about them.

The Countess Elvira had done her best to spread some negative stories about Gui. Almost every day, another story appeared somewhere either in print or on the Web. Kara, who rarely found herself in any society article, was now being actively courted by TMZ.com and *Hello!* magazine.

She had promised Katie that, if she suddenly

decided to be interviewed about her playboy fiancé, she'd give her an exclusive. But Kara wasn't interested in talking to anyone about Gui. Most articles about the two of them focused on their whirlwind courtship and the fact that Count Gui, as the press referred to him, was so enamored of her, he was demanding they be married in two weeks' time.

Which was precisely the truth. She and Rina were exhausting every resource they had to pull off a wedding so quickly. Even her father, who normally was nothing but reserved, commented that she'd waited long enough to find a man but that the wait seemed to have paid off.

She felt like a perfect fool. A fraud, really. She'd agreed to every demand that Gui had. The only thing she'd insisted on was that he couldn't look outside their marriage as long as they were happy together. Gui had finally consented when she'd flat-out refused to promise to not look at another man if he could look at any woman he wanted to.

She rubbed the back of her neck and pretended to look through the design book that the Sabina family had secured for her. It was filled with exclusive, one-of-a-kind wedding dresses that were worthy of a wedding of her fortune and Gui's. Cynthia brought over a stack of newspaper clippings and articles that mentioned her. One glaring headline made her want to toss them all in the trash bin.

The Spanish Aristocrat's Woman.

For God's sake, why did they insist on labeling her instead of using her name?

She skimmed the rest of the article and saw that it was full of inaccuracies, especially when it mentioned how she'd stolen him from his longtime lover...Elvira.

There was a photo of Elvira and her husband. She looked beautiful as always, and poor Juan looked angry and ready to deck the photographer. She wasn't sure what was between Elvira, Juan and Gui. He still wouldn't talk to her about it.

And she was trying to convince herself that she was okay with that. But the more articles she read that mentioned her new part in that old triangle, the more convinced she was that she needed to know what had happened between them all.

"You look tense," Gui said as he came up to her. "Turn toward the bulkhead, *bebe,* and I'll massage your shoulders."

She did what he asked and felt his big, warm hands on her shoulders. He massaged her with deep sure strokes. Her body responded instantly to his touch. She'd become accustomed to him touching and arousing her and then making love to her.

She knew she wasn't the most attractive woman in the world, but Gui didn't seem to realize that. He was enthralled with her and her body and made love to her often. At least three times a day. She'd never had this much sex before. Her thighs ached and her breasts felt fuller than they had been before he'd become her lover.

He leaned over her, reading the article on the top of the pile.

"Juan needs to control his temper."

"Why is he so angry all the time?"

Gui pressed a kiss to the spot where her neck and shoulder met. "I'm not sure."

"Gui?"

"Hmm?"

"Don't lie to me about this. If you don't want to say why, then just say that."

"What makes you think I'm lying?" he asked.

She turned in the seat so they were facing each other. "Your voice slips a little lower than usual when you aren't telling the entire truth."

He quirked one eyebrow at her. "I hadn't realized you'd picked up on that."

"Well, we've spent the last few days with each other 24/7. I think I'm getting to know you very intimately."

"Indeed you are, Kara. And I'm getting to know you intimately as well."

She shook her head, because she knew this tone, too. His voice only dropped this low when he wanted to have sex. "What do you know about me?"

He leaned down close, speaking directly into her ear. "I know that when I talk to you like this, you shiver for me. And your body starts to ready itself for mine.

"I know that when I kiss you right here—" he dropped a warm kiss behind her ear, making her squirm in her seat as wetness pooled between her legs "—you get wet."

"Gui—"

He tipped her head back and kissed her lingeringly, lifting his head only after they were both breathing heavily. "I know that you match my passions perfectly."

And she knew he was talking only about sex, but a part of her believed she matched his passions in other ways, too.

It was a start.

Seven

Kara didn't know what to think of Gui's family. After her own small one, his was a bit overwhelming. His sisters were very nice to her, and welcoming, but they had a lot of energy and big personalities. There were three of them.

She'd only met Arcelia and Anika, who were both in their late twenties. Augustina, Gui's youngest sister, was only sixteen and was back at boarding school in Switzerland. However, she would be joining the family for a party to celebrate Kara and Gui's engagement.

The two sisters she'd met were skinny and beautiful, and Kara felt fatter and plainer every second she was with them.

Cynthia was doing her level best to find legitimate work-related functions for Kara to attend but unfortunately this afternoon she had nothing on her schedule, so when Arcelia and Anika asked her to join them for an afternoon of shopping…she said yes.

Puerta del Sol was the center of Madrid and was considered by many to be the center of Spain. Every distance in the country was measured by how far it was from the crescent-shaped plaza in the center of Madrid. They shopped for three hours before making their way to a restaurant on the plaza where they decided to have a late lunch.

"How did Gui ask you to marry him?" Anika asked once they were seated and all had a glass of sangria.

Kara flushed. No one had asked these questions of her, because she'd neatly avoided being alone with her friends and her sister since the engagement had been announced. Now she was faced with either telling them the truth or making something up.

She took a sip of her fruity wine drink. "You know how Gui is. He didn't really ask me so much as tell me."

Arcelia started laughing. "Typical Gui. I hope you gave him a hard time for asking you like that."

"I did."

"Good for you. He always said he would never marry, and to be honest I was a bit surprised when I read about your engagement. Mother was furious that he didn't call and let us know first."

"I'm sorry you had to find out in the newspaper."

"It's okay. Gui isn't really big on communicating. You will have to be the one to keep us in the loop."

"So why do you think he asked you to marry him?" Anika asked.

"I have no idea," Kara said. Truly, she suspected it had something to do with Tristan and Christos both settling down.

"You're not his normal type of woman."

"I know," Kara said. She thought about that every day when she woke up in bed with Gui. Since they'd come to Madrid, he hadn't made love to her. And a part of her wondered if he had regrets now that they were here. Now that the wedding was only a few short days away.

Anika reached across the table and took her hand. "I think that's a good thing. He was dating these women who were…" She glanced at her sister, who shrugged.

"Shallow?"

"Yes, shallow. They were a bit trying at times. But you aren't like that."

"Well, thank you," Kara said.

Anika laughed. "I sound like a flake, don't I?"

"A little. What are you trying to say without saying it?" Kara was really starting to like Gui's sisters. They had that genuine core of solidness that she sensed in Gui. Kara suspected it was because of the way they'd all been raised. There was no room for doubt or weakness in their family. Gui's parents loved all of their children, and it was clear to see that that affection and support had helped those children to mature into adults with purpose.

"We'd like to help out with your foundation. As soon as Gui mentioned your name, we knew who you were. A&A Works has been looking for the right charity to partner with."

Kara smiled at the women. They owned their own jewelry design house. "What did you have in mind? I'd have to talk to Malcolm, who heads up our joint promotions department, but I'd love to create a one-of-a-kind piece of jewelry that we could sell and use the proceeds to fund a new housing development for women and children. Maybe here in Madrid."

"Yes, we have considered that before. But we want to be involved globally."

"Let me get you in touch with Malcolm and then you can figure something out. I'm thinking we could start with a series of exclusive bracelets each inspired by a different country, and then use the proceeds in that country."

Anika nodded and grabbed a pen to start jotting down notes. And Kara felt more like herself than she had since she'd arrived in Spain.

Gui had been busy working at Seconds and taking care of his own obligations, and Kara had been at loose ends feeling very much the outsider in her own new life.

But this was exactly the type of thing that she could sink her teeth into. "When I get back I'll e-mail Malcolm." She paused. "Thanks for inviting me to come shopping with you this afternoon."

"You're welcome. We figured you needed an afternoon of relaxation before tonight."

"Are royal functions that trying?" Kara asked. Gui had invited her to a dinner party at his brother's house. Gui's sister-in-law was the Enfanta...heir to the Spanish throne.

"They can be fun. But I suspected that Elvira will go out of her way to make you feel like an outsider."

Kara's skin suddenly felt too tight. Why hadn't Gui mentioned that the other woman would be there? Not that he had to. "I...I didn't realize she'd be there."

"The dinner is for the entire family to meet you. And Juan is our cousin through marriage."

She shook her head and smiled. "Well, I am looking forward to meeting all of your relatives."

Arcelia leaned forward. "Don't sweat it about Elvira. She's very good at playing games with men, but she tends to leave the women alone. She thinks the rest of us are below her."

That wasn't exactly reassuring. Kara knew she had to talk to Gui and find out exactly what was between him and the other woman. If she didn't have that knowledge, Elvira was always going to be able to rattle her and Kara didn't intend to give the older woman the ability to shake her up.

She was going to have to be at her best tonight. As lunch ended and she left Anika and Arcelia to head back to Gui's home, she decided that she was pulling out all the stops. She'd be the sexy woman that Gui told her she was, confident and proud to be on his arm.

That part was fine, but what caused the knot in the pit of her stomach was the fact that she'd have to somehow convince him that *he* was proud to be on *her* arm. Proud to be her man.

What she really wanted was to somehow make him realize that he was happy with her.

Gui had been busy since they'd landed in Madrid. Between his family business interests, running Seconds and taking care of all his social obligations, he'd had little time for Kara. This was his life, he thought and, for the first time, regretted it. He wanted to have time to simply make love to his woman and hold her in his arms.

"Count, I have laid out your suit for this evening. Your father has asked that you come early so that he can speak to you and Alonzo."

Gui nodded to Vincent as he took off the polo shirt he'd been wearing, tossing it toward the bed. "Inform my father I will be there. Will you let Kara know I'm home and if she has time I'd like to see her."

"I certainly will, Count. Is there anything else you need?"

"Please have the Bugatti brought around for us to take tonight."

"Very well, Count."

Vincent left and Gui went in to take a quick shower. He had little hope that Kara would be waiting when he came out. She'd kept herself incredibly busy since they'd landed in Spain. He was beginning to think she might have second thoughts about marrying him.

There was a knock on the door that led to Kara's dressing room. He wrapped a towel around his waist before going to open it. She stood on the other side, one arm wrapped around her waist, the other hanging by her side.

She had on more makeup than she normally wore and her dress was incredibly flattering. "You're gorgeous tonight, *bebe*."

She inclined her head. "Thank you, Gui. I'm glad you asked to speak to me. I need to talk to you, as well."

Kara was all business and he wondered what was going through her head. "About what?"

She came into his dressing room, taking a seat on the padded bench in the middle of the area. She carefully arranged her skirts, and it didn't take a genius to figure out what she was going to want to talk about.

"I need to know what's going on between you and Elvira and Juan. I know that you've said that it's all in the past, but everyone keeps mentioning her to me like I know what happened."

"It's really nothing to do with you," he said.

She blanched, and he wondered if she'd back down. He hoped she'd just let it go and that would be the end of it. He had absolutely no interest in re-hashing the past.

She shook her head. "If I weren't marrying you, I'd agree. But I am, and this is important to me, Gui. I can't continue on without knowing more about her."

"Why does it concern you?"

"Because she sent me a gift this afternoon, Gui."

"What did she send?"

"Intimate apparel," Kara said. There was an indefinable emotion on her face.

"I'm sorry. I have no idea why she would do that."

"Don't you? She said that the garment she sent was your favorite to see on the female form."

"Kara—"

"She was also thoughtful enough to include an exercise DVD that would help me to look better in it."

Gui cursed under his breath, crossing to Kara. "I hope you discarded both items."

"I did send them back," Kara said. "But I really can't continue to let this lie. I need to know the entire story."

"What do you want to know?" he asked her, reaching for his dress shirt. He drew it on and buttoned it quickly. He reached for the collar stays that Vincent left on his counter and put them into his shirt before drawing on his tie.

"I guess I want to know everything. From the beginning. Katie said she was the love of your life and she broke your heart."

Gui hated talking about Elvira. It meant remembering that time in his life when he was a bit out of control. When he'd been young and impetuous and ruled by passion and not logic.

It wasn't that he was totally logical now, but he was in better control of his temper. And he'd never be as all-or-nothing now as he'd been back then.

"Elvira and I met the summer after I finished at university. Tristan, Christos and I were taking a gap year."

"Isn't that a bit late?"

"Yes, but we'd decided that the normal rules didn't apply to us. It was actually our second gap year. We did the traditional one between prep school and university as well."

"How did you meet her?"

"I met her in Stockholm. We were there for three months, and she and I had a passionate affair. When it was time to move on, I went with my friends. Elvira followed me and two weeks later we moved to Madrid together. She had a villa that had been left to her by her grandfather. And I was on the outs with my father at the time, so we lived there.

"We lived together for three months before I got restless and joined Tristan and Christos in Milan. Elvira married Juan after I left. That's it. Not much of a story."

"What were you restless about?" Kara asked. And Gui realized that was the real treasure to Kara. That she seemed to always be able to look deep into the heart of a person. Not just listen to the surface story but dig beyond. No one had ever paid attention to what he said the way she did when it came to personal stuff.

"I was thinking about marrying her, but I was young and had to be sure."

"Oh, Gui."

"Don't pity me. I came back to Madrid, unsure if she was the woman for me. And finding her married to Juan convinced me she wasn't."

Kara wasn't sure what she'd expected from Gui, but this story wasn't it. She'd expected… She had no idea. There was more to the story. There had to be, but her heart broke thinking of him coming back to marry Elvira and finding her with another man: Married to someone else.

"I don't pity you."

She almost pitied Elvira, because it was clear from the story that the other woman had had no idea where she'd stood with Gui. Something that Kara herself felt. Gui wasn't one of those men who spoke freely about his emotions.

He wanted her. She knew that from how often he made love to her. But she thought relationships should be about more than sex. They should include long conversations and romantic gestures. They should include…well, the other things that Gui did.

"Why are you looking at me like that?"

"I'm trying to figure you out."

"With me, you get what you see," he said, taking his dinner jacket and donning it.

"There is so much more to you than meets the eye, Guillermo. You just don't let anyone see more."

He didn't respond, holding his hand out to her. "Come here."

"Why?"

"I want to see how we look together."

She shook her head. "Not yet. I want to finish our discussion."

"It is finished, Kara. Elvira thought she could manipulate me into marrying her. I refused, she married someone else, and that's the end of it. I'm Catholic. Do you know what that means?"

"That you have a special dispensation from the Pope to miss church?" she asked in a teasing tone, because she hadn't seen him go to church once since they'd met unless she counted Tristan's wedding.

"Very funny. No, it means that I take the bonds of marriage very seriously. Elvira knew this about me."

"I know it, too," she said, remembering the conversation they'd had that first morning after they'd made love.

"Indeed you do," he said, coming over to her and

holding out his hand. She put her left hand in his, saw the large sapphire-cut diamond-and-platinum engagement ring he'd given her. No matter what Elvira wanted, Kara was the one who was engaged to Gui and she didn't intend to let him go.

What she intended, she realized as she rose to her feet and let him slip his arms around her, was to teach him to love her. And there was only one way to do that. She had to stop holding herself back. She had to be the woman she really was. The woman she'd been afraid to let him see because she was different from the other women of their social set.

Days of shopping and lunching weren't enough for her. And after spending time with Anika and Arcelia today, she had a hunch that Gui would be able to accept that other part of her.

She'd been feeling so lucky that he wanted her to marry him that she'd been hiding herself, not wanting to rock the boat. And that wasn't who she was.

"You're looking very fierce, *bebe.*"

"Sorry. I just realized something important."

"That Elvira is ancient history and you have nothing to worry about when it comes to her?"

She shook her head. "She still wants you."

Gui didn't deny it. "We look good together."

She looked at them in the mirror. Gui was a big man, tall and muscular and, standing next to him, she didn't look too big the way she did with men who were her height. Even though she wore heels, he still was taller than she was. He wrapped an arm around her waist and drew her back against his body, resting his chin on her shoulder.

For a split second she saw that fairy-tale couple. Gui filled the bill of handsome prince easily and for once she felt like she was the princess.

He kissed the base of her neck and she sighed, tipping her head back and looking up at him.

"What do you want, *querida?*"

"You," she said. "You've been too busy since we got here."

"I have been. I want you, too," he said, sliding his hand down to her tummy and pressing her back against his groin. She felt his erection nudge her lower back.

She shivered delicately and shifted against him. "But there's no time now."

"There's always time for making love to my fiancée."

She turned in his arms, rising up on her toes to kiss him. His mouth opened over hers and she felt that knot of uncertainty that had been in her stomach since her lunch with Gui's sisters start to melt.

Many couples met in ways that were unconventional, and Lord knows that people married for reasons nowhere near as sensible as hers and Gui's. And they had passion. The kind of passion she'd always believed was only found in movies or romance novels.

He sucked her lower lip between his teeth and she moaned in her throat. God she wanted this man. He leaned down to whisper in explicit terms what he wanted to do with her.

She flushed at the words, a pulse of pure pleasure going through her body. She arched against him.

"Yes, Gui. Take me like that."

He smiled down at her and then lifted her in his arms and carried her into his bedroom. He made love to her on the edge of the bed, thrusting deeply into her body and joining them so deeply that it was easy for her to believe that they'd never be apart. He called her name when he came, and as her own climax washed over her, she clung tightly to his shoulders, held him to her and vowed that she'd never let him go. That she'd find the way to ensure that together they'd have the happiness that she'd always felt was waiting for her with the right man.

With this man, she thought.

Eight

The house of the Enfanta Isabella and Alonzo was big and impressive, exactly what one would expect of the residence of the heiress to the throne. It was far and away the most impressive private home she'd seen, and she'd visited many.

Kara was a little intimidated as they pulled up in front of the house and a doorman came to open her door. She fumbled to open her purse and Gui waved the liveried man off. Though she'd met heads of state and spent her entire life around the privileged set, this was different. She was meeting Gui's family, really meeting them for the first time. And this party was in her and Gui's honor. Her first official function as his fiancée. Oh. My. God. She took a deep breath but it didn't help. Neither did the second or third one she tried.

"What's the matter, *mi dulce?*"

"Nothing," she said, hoping for once that he'd just let her get away with the white lie. She closed her eyes, trying to let his deep voice wash away her nerves. It did help a little.

"Kara, I know you better than that."

"Dang it. Can't you let it go this time?"

"No, I can't. Everything about you matters to me."

She wanted to believe him but Gui was used to romancing women and... Why did she do that to herself? She knew she was important to Gui. He wouldn't be planning to marry her if she didn't matter on one level or another. And they wouldn't be here in front of his sister-in-law and brother's home otherwise.

"Talk to me, *bebe.* Where is the confident woman who seduced me in my dressing room?"

She flushed. "I didn't seduce you. I was just sitting there."

He leaned over, his fingers brushing over her face before his mouth found hers. "That's all it takes to seduce me."

She smiled, feeling the confidence that came from the sexy feelings Gui evoked in her.

He kissed her again and she didn't want to stop. In his arms she forgot about meeting other people and what their opinions of her might be.

"What are you thinking about?" Gui asked, pulling back.

She shrugged. "Your family is filled with gorgeous people and they are used to socializing with other royals and I'm…"

"What are you?"

"Not what they are probably expecting from your fiancée."

"Didn't you spend the afternoon shopping with my sisters?"

"Yes."

"Did you enjoy it?"

"Yes."

He looked at her expectantly.

"That was different. Your sisters are very nice and they wanted to like me."

"Kara."

"Hmm?"

"What is going on in that beautiful head of yours?" he asked.

She smiled. She really couldn't help it. Each time he complimented her about her looks and body, she was filled with a rush of joy that she knew was unrealistic. "I'm not beautiful, Gui. That's the problem. I'm not going to fit in with this crowd."

"Kara, *mi dulce,* I don't want to hear anything else like that from your mouth. You are extremely good-looking and I will be the envy of every man in the room tonight."

She rolled her eyes and tried to think of something to say to convince Gui of what she meant. But he leaned forward and kissed her before she could think. It wasn't just a brush of the lips but was filled with passion.

She forgot everything. Her worries and fears, her doubts that she'd fit in at this function. Her fear that she wasn't enough for Gui.

Instead she put her hands around his shoulders and held on to him. Let the passion he called easily from her body overwhelm her. And she didn't have any doubts about where she belonged or how she looked when his arms were around her.

He pulled back. "Now you really do need to fix your lipstick."

"Gui?"

"*Si?*"

"Are you sure about marrying me? It's not too late to change your mind," she said, because for a long time those words had been in the back of her mind. Actually, she worried that she'd wake from this dream and find that she'd imagined everything. That she wasn't really in Madrid with Count Guillermo, and she wasn't going to be his wife.

"Kara, look at me."

She raised her eyes and met his gaze. The quiet confidence she saw in his gave her strength. It was moments like this that made her believe that she was going to find love and happiness with Gui.

"I'm not going to change my mind. We've made a commitment to each other and I intend to honor it."

She swallowed and blinked so the tears that burned the back of her eyes wouldn't fall. "Good. I intend to do the same."

"Then we are agreed," he said, then cursed under his breath.

"What's wrong?"

"My father has come out of the house. He must have heard us pull up."

"Oh, no. Do you think he saw us kissing?"

"Who cares?" Gui said.

"I do. Your father has published several articles on decorum, and public displays of affection are—"

"Perfectly acceptable between an engaged couple. My father would be surprised if we weren't touching each other."

"But still."

"But nothing. Ready to get out and meet the family and all my friends?"

She shook her head, but then he gave her one of his hot, sexy looks from under his eyebrows and she realized she *was* ready. With Guillermo by her side, she could do anything.

Gui sat with his brother, Alonzo, on the balcony overlooking Madrid. Their father, who had asked to see them alone before dinner, was still inside taking a last-minute call. There were cigars and Cuarenta Y Tres, which his father loved. The traditional Spanish liqueur was made from forty-three different fruits and herbs. It was something he only drank with Lonzo and his father.

Lonzo handed him a shot glass as the sun set. There was a peace and quietness between them. Unlike his friend Christos, who'd had a contentious relationship with his late older brother, Gui and Lonzo had always been two peas in a pod.

Before settling down to marriage, Lonzo had been just as wild as Gui was. Often they'd partied and run together. But all of that had changed when Lonzo married at twenty-five.

"I like your fiancée, Gui. How on earth did you find her?"

"I'm not incapable of finding a smart, beautiful woman, Lonzo."

"I'm aware of that, but normally you are incapable of keeping her for very long."

"You're just jealous because you've been an old married man for all of your life."

"Niños." They both stood at the sound of their father's voice.

"Papa."

"Thank you for coming early," he said and took a deep breath.

Gui put his drink down as did Lonzo. "Is everything okay?"

"Yes," he said, but there was something in his voice.

"Papa, what is it?" Gui asked, going over to his father.

"Don't worry, *mi hijo.* Your mama is having some health problems."

"What kind?" Lonzo asked.

"We're not sure. She's going in to see Dr. Gonzales in the morning for some tests and we'll know more."

"What are her symptoms?"

"She has had blinding headaches for the last three days and has been dizzy and tired, and that's not your mama."

"No it isn't. What time will you be done at the doctor?"

"By the afternoon."

"I'm going out of town tomorrow morning, Papa," Lonzo said. "Flying to Paris with Bella for a function. Should I cancel and stay here?"

"No. It's just a doctor appointment."

"I'll go with you."

"That's not necessary, Gui."

"It is to me," Gui said, glancing at Lonzo. His brother nodded. In this they were like one. They'd always take care of their family first. It was what they did. What their papa had done, and how they had been raised.

"Your mama insists this night be about you and your lovely Kara. So I haven't said anything to your sisters."

"Of course. We'll have a toast and make this night a special one so Mama doesn't worry," Lonzo said. "But Bella will know something is wrong."

Gui smiled to himself. Lonzo and Bella had one of those rare marriages where they truly were each other's best friend. Gui wondered if that was why he'd never married—he'd never found a woman who suited him the way that Bella suited Lonzo.

In the back of his mind was a thought about Kara,

but he brushed it aside. He didn't want to think about her beyond sex and marriage.

There was a rap on the door and he glanced up to see Vincent standing there.

"*Si*, Vincent?"

"Anika has asked to see you for a moment when you are finished here. She said it's about Miss Kara."

"Thank you, Vincent. Where is she waiting?"

"In the hallway."

Gui knew Kara was uncomfortable in large groups, but he'd left her in the capable hands of his sisters, sister-in-law and mother. No one else should have arrived yet.

"Excuse me, Papa, Lonzo."

His father chuckled. "The throes of new love are very exciting."

"Indeed, Papa."

They set a time to check in on the results of his mother's tests, and then Gui walked away from his brother and father, thinking how lucky he was to have them. His family had always been solid, filled with a kind of love that was unexplainable to outsiders.

Being with Kara brought him something close to the serenity he'd found in his family. Which concerned him. Despite his comments to Lonzo, he knew there was a reason he'd always moved on. And he wondered sometimes how he'd been lucky enough to make Kara his fiancée. Because at the end of the day, she really was too good for him.

Kara told herself that Elvira's comments had absolutely no reflection on her. That being called *feo* wasn't that bad. She knew she wasn't beautiful like Gui, but being called ugly to her face…

Elvira probably didn't realize she spoke Spanish fluently. Or maybe the other woman simply didn't care that she'd insulted Kara to her face.

Arcelia had defended Kara, telling Elvira to back off or she'd be asked to leave. But Kara hadn't stayed. She'd had enough of Elvira.

The other woman was truly one of the most gorgeous women that Kara had ever seen, but that beauty was only skin-deep. Before Elvira had approached Kara, she'd heard the countess make snide remarks around others in the room. Then, when Gui's mother had entered the room, Elvira had suddenly turned all cooing and nice. She'd even stopped speaking Spanish and had addressed Kara in English.

But by that point Kara had decided it was time to get some fresh air. So here she was in the lush garden courtyard, accompanied by only a fountain and the scent of the blooms in the air.

Her dress, which had seemed so perfect tonight,

no longer had the power to make her feel pretty. Instead she felt as she always did, too big and too awkward to really be a princess. To really be a part of the social set that she'd been born into.

She should go back to the party before anyone realized she left. Instead, she followed the cobblestone path around to the fountain and a padded bench nestled under a large fruit tree.

She brushed the seat off before sitting down. Wrapping her arms around her waist, she held herself and closed her eyes.

She needed to find her confidence. She pictured Rina and tried to infuse herself with the attitude her sister always carried around. She heard Rina's voice in her mind, telling her that she was a deMontaine and that when people made ignorant remarks about her looks or size, it was due to jealousy.

But that didn't help right now. Because Elvira's comments hadn't just been about her looks, but about her own secret fears where Gui was concerned. Maybe she really wasn't good enough for him.

Maybe…

"*Bebe,* why are you out here alone?"

She opened her eyes. "I needed some fresh air. How did you find me? I thought you were meeting with your father and brother."

"I was. We were finished and Anika came to find me."

She flushed a little. She'd truly hoped that it had just been Arcelia who'd heard Elvira's comments. "Why?"

"She was concerned about you."

"I'm fine," she said.

"But you aren't."

"Gui, I need you to let this lie. I'm finding my center and I'm going to be able to go back in there and function. But if you make me talk about this, I'm going to cry—"

He cut her words off with a kiss. It wasn't about passion—she felt something different. She felt, as silly as it sounded even to her, that he was wrapping her in the affection he held for her. He made her feel beautiful and confident. He pulled back a second later and she forced a smile to her lips.

"That was very nice. Let's go back to the party now."

"Not yet, *mi dulce*."

"Gui…"

He lifted her off the bench and sat down, settling her on his lap. He gently pushed her head down on his shoulder and wrapped his arms around her.

"Until you believe in yourself, people like Elvira are always going to have power over you."

"I do believe in myself," she said.

"Yes, you do, until you meet someone you perceive as being physically better-looking than you are."

She shrugged. She couldn't deny it. Her weight and size were always in the back of her mind, making her feel awkward. They always had.

"I can't change that."

He tipped her chin up so that he was looking down into her face and she caught her breath, not even hearing the words he said. He was so handsome and sexy, and she realized why Elvira's comments bothered her so much.

Gui deserved a woman who was truly his equal. Truly the other half of him. A woman whom everyone would glance at and know was his wife or fiancée.

"Did you hear what I said?"

She shook her head. "You are so handsome."

He laughed. "That's neither here nor there. You are the one whose beauty has captivated me. I need you to believe that, Kara."

"When you hold me, I do."

"Then know that I'm always holding you," he said.

She smiled and tried to make it real. Tried to make it come from deep inside, but that was difficult. Because deep in her soul she knew that, no matter what Gui said to the rest of the world, they'd always be an odd couple. Gorgeous Gui and his fat fiancée.

Tears burned her eyes and she blinked rapidly, but he'd already seen them.

He cursed under his breath and then leaned down to kiss her. Really kiss her this time. His tongue thrust deep in her mouth and his hands tightened on her body until she was a mass of need and desire for him.

She felt his body stir under her hip.

"You need to start believing me when I tell you that you are the only woman who arouses me so quickly."

She shifted in his arms, wrapping her own around his shoulders, and realized how ridiculous she'd been to let Elvira's comments ruin her evening. This night was about her and Gui, and for once she needed to let go of everything else and just focus on that.

Nine

Gui drove the sleek Bugatti sports car through the streets of Madrid. The dinner at his brother's house had been nice once Elvira and Juan left. They'd stayed only for the cocktail hour. Twice Gui had had a moment to be alone with his old lover, and both times he felt... He didn't know what he felt. But it was different than it had always been before.

And looking over at Kara sitting next to him in the leather bucket seat of the world's fastest production car, he realized that he wanted what she brought to his life. She slowed him down. She eased the restlessness that had always been so much a part of him. He didn't understand how to stop and stand still.

The moon was full tonight, and the light spilled into the car and over Kara's smooth skin. She had her head back against the seat and her face was turned toward him. Her full lips were curved in a smile.

The gentleness of Kara was something that always took him by surprise. Even his sisters and mother, whom he adored, were passionate creatures with volatile tempers, but Kara was peaceful and soothing.

"Your brother is pretty funny and very charming. But that didn't surprise me."

"I taught him everything he knows," Gui said.

"I think your father did. I really liked him. He told me once we were married I could call him Poppy."

"Did he? He likes you, Kara."

"I'm glad. I was worried about that. Your sisters are really nice. They're going to do some work with my foundation back in the States."

"Why did you start a foundation?"

"My mother. She died of breast cancer when I was a teen. We were fine, of course, because of my father's money, but Rina and I met other kids whose families weren't well off, and they were struggling to survive after losing their mothers. It may sound silly, but at sixteen I told my father that when I grew up I was going to make sure that families who went through what we did had a nice place to live."

He smiled over at her. "That doesn't sound silly at all. It sounds very much like you, *mi dulce.*"

"I guess you're right. The need to help others is a big part of who I am. Don't get me wrong, I like a shopping trip as much as the next girl. I just need to feel like I have a purpose."

"I, too, am like that," Gui said.

"Why did you choose to work with kids? You didn't lose a parent."

"No, I didn't. But I did form a tight bond with my mates when I was thirteen. Tristan and Christos and I became friends because we were forced to be in each other's company at school."

"Forced?"

"Um…not sure what the right word for it is in English, but we were in trouble a lot and were given demerits and sent to work in the stables and on the grounds together."

"Why am I not surprised that you three were troublemakers?" she asked with a soft laugh.

"I like your laugh, Kara."

"You do?"

"Yes. It always makes me smile."

She smiled over at him with the hint of innocence and shyness that he associated only with her.

"Tell me more about how you turned trouble-making into an idea for helping kids."

He downshifted for a traffic light and brought the car to a stop. He put his hand on Kara's thigh, and she shifted her legs toward him as he slid his hand upward.

"We became mates because we did stuff together and we shared the same disdain for authority. That gave me the idea that the kids who were getting into trouble in Madrid were probably in the same situation we were. Not enough of the right kind of activity."

"That makes sense. Too much free time is never good when you're young."

"Did you get into trouble?"

"No. I'm a rule follower. I like to know what the boundaries are and to stay within them."

"I like to know where the boundaries are, too," he said, shifting the car into gear when the light changed. Kara lifted her hand to his and he joined their fingers together and held them loosely on the gearshift.

"Yes, but you blow right past the limits, don't you? Even as an adult you still don't like to follow the rules."

"How do you know that?"

She arched one eyebrow at him. "You must be

kidding. I'm engaged to you because you told me I am."

That startled a laugh out of him. She was relaxed, teasing him. And he was seeing a woman...a woman he never wanted to let go.

That was another nice thing about marriage, he thought. For the first time, he realized that regular sex wasn't the only plus to being married. There was also this quiet conversation. This teasing between the two of them.

He lifted their joined hands to his mouth and kissed her knuckles.

"What are you thinking?" she asked.

He noticed she did that a lot. For some reason, she wanted to know what made him tick. But he wasn't about to tell her what he was thinking now, because those kinds of thoughts left him too vulnerable.

She'd become important to him, and how the hell had that happened? She was a woman he was marrying so that he wasn't the odd man out with his friends. She was the woman he was using to get Elvira out of his system and to finally, after ten long years, move on.

Kara was the woman who was supposed to be there when he needed her. And he was supposed to only need her for sex and for social functions. But, holding her hand in his, he realized he needed her for *this*. This quiet sharing in the middle of the night was just as important as the other reasons.

And he came to realize in that instant that he really did need her, and he wasn't ever going to let her go.

Kara didn't know what to expect when they got home, but after the way he'd kissed her in the car, it wasn't to separate in the foyer. But Vincent was waiting for them, and she knew that something must be important for Gui's secretary to be waiting up for them at one-thirty in the morning.

"I'll see you upstairs?"

"Si, bebe," he said, kissing her lingeringly.

She pulled away reluctantly and looked back at him just once before hurrying up the elegant staircase. She opened the door to her bedroom and walked inside, trying to tell herself that this romance was all in her head. That what she and Gui had was about convenience, both of them needing and wanting marriage for business reasons. It had nothing to do with romance.

Except, on this moonlit night, it sure didn't feel that way to her.

She opened the door to her balcony and stepped outside into the cool spring evening. The moon was full and bright and she lifted her hand to cup it.

Holding the moon in her hand... Was that like

fooling herself into believing that she and Gui had real romance between them?

"Bebe?"

"Out here," she said.

He walked out onto the balcony. He'd shed his dinner jacket and tie before joining her.

"Is everything okay?"

"Yes. I need to call Tristan first thing in the morning."

"Oh?"

"Seconds business. We had to fire one of our finance officers recently for embezzling."

"I don't understand why someone would steal."

"You wouldn't," he said and drew her into his arms, kissing her the way he did.

And immediately she caught fire. One touch of his mouth on hers was all it took to arouse her. It didn't help matters that her entire body was still tingling from the orgasm he'd given her before they left for the dinner party.

He nibbled on her lips and held her still when she would have undulated against him. She lifted her hands to his shoulders, burying her hands in the crisp hair at the back of his neck.

His mouth left hers and she felt the gentle scrape of his teeth against her neck. She dug her nails into his shoulders.

He caressed her back and spine. She rubbed herself against him, wishing they were both naked. "Let's go inside."

"Not yet," he said, finding the tab of her zipper and drawing it down. The cool evening air brushed over her skin. He pushed the dress off her shoulders and it fell down her hips to pool at her feet. She glanced down at the body she'd always felt was unfashionable.

Gui tipped her head up to his. "You are exquisite, *querida*. I want to see you wearing nothing but moonlight and my ring."

She nodded. He unfastened the back clasp of her bra and drew the fabric away from her breasts. Her nipples were already beaded with arousal and tightened more as the cool air touched them.

Gui cupped her breasts, running his finger over her nipples. He brushed his finger back and forth until she bit her lower lip and shifted in his arms.

"Now take off your panties, *bebe*."

She reached for the waistband of her panties, pushed them down her hips and let them fall down her legs. She stepped out of them and then out of her shoes. She had nothing on now, just the moonlight that bathed the city and this night in its magical glow. And, of course, the ring on her left hand.

"Stand over there," he said. She stepped to where

he'd indicated. He sank down in the padded rocking chair on the balcony and just stared at her.

"What are you doing?" she asked, starting to remember she wasn't svelte.

"God, woman, you are so beautiful."

"Gui."

"Come here so I can make love to my fiancée."

She walked over to him slowly and he pulled her onto his lap. The rocking chair was large enough to seat two people, so straddling him was easy for her.

He cupped her breasts again and she moaned before he touched her nipples. He leaned down and caught the tip of one breast between his lips, drawing her into his mouth and suckling her.

She held his shoulders and moved on him, rubbing her center over his erection.

He scraped his fingernail over her nipple and she shivered in his arms. She drew back a little bit so she could see him. Her breasts were bare, nipples distended and begging for his mouth. He lowered his head and suckled her some more.

He held her still with a hand on the small of her back. He buried his other hand in her hair and arched her over his arm. Both of her breasts were thrust up at him.

"Damn, you are so hot tonight."

Her eyes closed and her hips moved subtly

against him. When he blew on her nipple, goose-flesh spread down her body.

She loved how hot he made her. Loved how open and honest he was with his reactions to her body. Loved his mouth on her breasts. Her nipples were so sensitive and she felt everything in her body clenching.

He leaned down and licked the valley between her breasts. She remembered the last time he'd left his mark on her right there. He hadn't done that since the first time they'd made love.

He kept kissing and rubbing, caressing her nipples until her hands clenched in his hair and she rocked her hips harder against his length. He lifted his hips, thrusting up against her and then biting carefully on one tender, aroused nipple. She cried his name and he covered her mouth with his. She sucked his tongue into her mouth, needing to make him feel the same out-of-control passion that was swamping her right now.

He rocked her until she quieted in his arms, then he held her close. She felt him between her legs through the fabric of his pants and realized that, once again, he was still dressed.

She glanced up at him and saw he was watching her. The fire in his eyes made her entire body tight with anticipation. He lifted her into his arms and carried her into the bedroom. Laying her on the center of the bed, he unzipped his pants and pushed them down his legs. He opened the top drawer of the nightstand and grabbed a condom, putting it on one-handed before turning back to her.

"Hurry," she said. The doubts that had plagued her all her life were gone. She knew that this man liked her body. This sexy, virile man wanted her, and no other woman could satisfy him the way she could.

"Not a chance. I'm going to savor you."

"Betcha can't," she said, reaching out to caress him. He groaned and fell forward, catching his weight on his arms.

"You really want—"

"I really want you, Gui. Deep inside me now."

"How do you want me, *bebe?*"

She wrapped her arms around his neck and lifted herself up to kiss him hard on the lips. Then whispered in his ear how she wanted him.

Hearing in explicit detail what she wanted from him seemed to inflame him, and he fell on her. She wrapped her arms and legs around him as he shifted his body. She felt him at the entrance to her body, and then he thrust home, all the way inside of her. So deep she felt like they'd always be connected this way.

She smiled up at him. "Don't try to last, honey. Make me yours."

He hugged her close and then took her mouth, thrusting his tongue between her lips in the same rhythm as he thrust into her body. She wrapped her thighs high around his waist. Her hands fluttered between them, and their eyes met.

He held her hips steady and thrust deeply, his pace increasing as their passion grew frenzied. Her eyes widened with each inch he gave her. She clutched at his hips, holding him to her.

He leaned down and caught one of her nipples in his teeth, scraping very gently. She started to tighten around him. Her hips moved faster, demanding more, but he kept the pace slow, steady. She didn't want to come again without him.

He suckled her nipple and shifted his hips to catch her pleasure point with each thrust. She clutched her hands in his hair and threw her head back as another climax ripped through her.

"Gui," she said. "Come with me, honey."

"Not yet. I want you crazy with pleasure."

"I *am*."

He varied his thrusts, finding a rhythm that made her shiver again. She knew she was going to come again and this time she wanted him with her. She loved when they were together like this. It was the only time that she felt truly like they were both honest with each other.

He leaned back on his haunches and tipped her hips up to give him deeper access to her body. Then she scraped her nails down his back, clutching his buttocks and drawing him in. She felt him thrust harder and faster and knew his orgasm was near. She looked up at his face and felt everything in the world narrow to this one man. She knew then that she loved him.

He called her name as he came, and she felt her own body answer with another orgasm. She wrapped her arms around him and held him close.

She wanted to drift off to sleep in his arms before she did something truly silly and blurted out how much she loved him.

Ten

Gui wasn't in the best mood as he drove through rush hour traffic in Madrid. He was supposed to meet Kara thirty minutes ago for a meeting with the caterer for their wedding. And though he couldn't care less what food was served at the reception, it was the one thing that Kara had asked him to give his opinion on and he'd wanted to make it on time.

But the day wasn't going to plan. And he'd had to deal with three different calls from Juan. The man was determined to seek him out. The last thing he wanted to do was have a meeting with a man who wanted to discuss Elvira, and it was clear that was all that Juan wanted. Thank goodness he was going with Alonzo and Bella on one of their frequent goodwill trips today.

Gui's mobile phone rang and he glanced at the caller ID. It was an official number from the palace. "De Cuaron."

"Count de Cuaron, this is Señor Montoyes. There has been an accident."

He hit the brakes and pulled over to the shoulder. "Is my brother okay?"

"We're not sure yet, Count."

"When will you be sure?"

"Shortly. Will you be at your residence?"

"Yes. I will be at my residence." He took a long breath. "Where was the accident?"

"Outside of Paris. The royal family's jet has crashed."

"Survivors?"

"We don't know yet."

"What do you know?"

"Only what I've told you. We wanted to get word to the family before you heard it on the television."

"Thank you, Montoyes. Call me as soon as you hear something."

"Of course, I will."

He hung up the phone and realized he was shaking. He couldn't imagine a world without his older brother in it. Goddamn. He pulled back into the slow-moving traffic, then maneuvered his car off the motorway and found a quiet side street on which to stop the car.

He took several deep breaths and tried to figure out something he could do. But nothing immediately came to mind. He dialed Kara's cell phone number.

"Gui?"

"*Si.*"

"Did the Palace reach you?"

"*Si.*"

"Oh, my. I'm so sorry. I don't know what's going on, but I have a call in to Katie, who has an office in Paris. And I've got every TV in the house tuned to a different news channel. The Americans aren't covering it yet, but the French channel is, as is Skye TV in the UK."

"What are they saying?"

"Just that a jet carrying the Enfanta and her entourage has crashed. That's it. They don't even know right now if there are survivors."

He tightened his grip on the phone. He breathed through his nose, refusing to give in to the emotions that were threatening. He wasn't a man given to tears, but to lose his brother and sister-in-law would be a hard blow.

"Where are you?"

He glanced up and down the street. "I have no idea."

"Do you have your GPS on?"

"What? Yes, I do."

"Give me the address and I'll send Vincent for you. I don't think you should drive right now."

"Don't be ridiculous. Of course I can drive. I'll be home in—" he glanced down at the GPS directional unit and saw that he was very close to his house "—in a few minutes. I'm going to need to get on the phone when I get there."

"I know. I'll help you in any way I can."

"Have my parents been notified?"

"Yes. I spoke to Anika a few minutes ago. Everyone is gathering at your parents' house if you want to go there."

"Thank you, Kara."

"You don't have to thank me. This is what being part of a couple is all about."

He hung up and started the car again. Kara's words rang in his head. Being a couple was one thing; being concerned for each other's well-being was different. This was the reason he'd been reluctant to marry for so long. How could he have forgotten that?

Marrying because Christos and Tristan had

wasn't good enough. Marrying because it was past time that he got over Elvira wasn't valid either. He had avoided marrying because when he lived alone he could deal with things the way he wanted to. And right now, he wanted to point the Bugatti in any direction that would take him out of Madrid and away from the situation with his brother.

God, how had Christos borne the death of Stavros, his older brother? His friend had been estranged from his brother at the time of Stavros's death but, all the same, he must have felt the same gaping hole in his life that Gui felt at this moment.

His mobile rang again. No number was displayed on the caller ID. He answered it and heard a ragged sob on the other end of the phone.

"De Cauron."

"Gui, *querido*. Can you come to my house?"

"Why, Elvira?"

"Juan was traveling with the Enfanta and I just had news that he's dead."

"Who called you? Have they confirmed that anyone else is dead?"

"Just my Juan. I need you, Gui. Come to me," she said. Her sobs echoed over the line, and then they were cut off. Gui dialed the Palace office and got a busy signal. He called his home and got Vincent, who told him he hadn't heard anything else about Alonzo.

Gui was torn between wanting to go home and going to Elvira. For ten years he'd waited for her to need him and now she did, and he wondered why he was even contemplating going to her, but he turned the car in the direction of her home and drove to her house.

Kara was sick with worry when Gui didn't show up at the house. Three hours later, she realized he must have gone somewhere else. Vincent hadn't spoken to him and she'd tried to call only once and got his voice mail. She had left a message and knew she couldn't call back. She didn't want to nag him or be a pest.

But she was concerned about him. And she had no idea what she should do. Should she stay at his house and wait for him or head over to his parents' house where the rest of his family was? And was she part of the family now? They weren't even married yet. She really needed Gui here to tell her what to do.

Her cell phone rang and she almost dropped it trying to answer it quickly. "This is Kara."

"It's Katie."

"What's up? Did you hear any more news?"

"Yes. Alonzo is fine, as is the Enfanta."

"That's a relief. I can't wait to tell Gui."

"Where is he?"

"Not home yet."

"Um…there was one death, Kara."

"Who?"

"The Enfanta's cousin, Juan de Perez."

Did Gui know that? She rubbed the back of her neck, feeling way too tired to try to figure out anything else tonight. "Thanks, Katie, for getting this information for me."

"You're welcome. It'll be showing up on the television pretty soon. We just had everything confirmed and we're running the story."

"Do they know what happened to the plane?"

"Not yet. There's been speculation that it was some kind of mechanical failure."

"Right." She didn't know what else to say. She wanted to talk to her friend about Gui and how their relationship had been strengthening, but tonight she wasn't sure that was still the case.

"I can't believe you're getting married in less than a week."

She swallowed hard and knew that this was one of those moments that would divide her life. Like her mother's death had. There had been the years with her mom, and then the years without. And this was going to be the dividing line between when she'd been engaged to Gui and whatever happened afterward.

A part of her knew she was borrowing trouble,

but another part was convinced that Juan's death and Gui's absence at home were tied to each other.

"I'm not sure that the wedding will take place as scheduled. Especially since there will be a funeral to attend."

"I hadn't thought of that. Let me know if you need me to do anything."

"I will."

"I mean it, Kara. This is probably going to be a hard time for Gui and his family, and I know how you try to take care of everyone. Lean on me if you need to."

"Seriously, Katie. If I feel like I need someone, I will call you."

"Good. Now go have a drink and try to unwind. Please give my condolences to Gui and his family."

"I will. Thanks again for helping me out."

"No problem, hon."

Kara started to disconnect the line.

"Is everything else okay? With you and Gui?"

She took a deep breath. Intensely private, she kept most of the details of her personal life even from her friends. And right now, when she had a bunch of doubts and fears racing around her mind about Gui, she didn't want to talk to anyone. Even Katie.

"Yes, everything's fine. Just a little wired from the news of the crash and worrying about it being Gui's brother. I met him last week."

"I heard. Gossip has it that you charmed every-one in the royal family."

"Well, I don't know if that's true, but I did have a good time." Eventually.

"I'm sure it is true. You can be very vivacious when you forget to worry."

"Is that a compliment?" she asked her friend, relaxing a little as they bantered back and forth. This was what she needed. Madrid was fine and a nice place to live when she had Gui by her side but she needed her girlfriends.

"Yes, it is. You need tough love."

"Ha. You have a razor-sharp tongue, which is why you work in the gossipmonger industry."

"Oh, so you're going to hit me there after I just used my gossipmongering ways to help you out?"

"You know I was kidding."

"Yes, I do."

Kara wandered down the hallway to Gui's den and stood on the threshold of his private sanctuary before going inside. She didn't turn on any lights, just let the illumination from the hallway lead her way. She walked to his big leather chair and sat down in it.

"Kara?"

"Hmm?"

"Are you sure you're okay?"

"Yes. I'm fine. The entire last two weeks of my life have been so fast. You know?"

"Yes, I do. You're not really a speed of light kind of person."

"Normally I'd agree, but with Gui…"

"Do you love him?"

She sighed. "Would I be marrying him if I didn't?"

"I guess not. You aren't the kind of person to marry because it makes sense."

Funny that Katie had summed up the lie she'd been telling herself since she'd agreed to be Gui's fiancée. Why was it that her friends could see the obvious and she couldn't?

She heard the front door open and Gui's deep voice downstairs. "Gui's home, Katie. I'll call you back later."

"Okay, Kara."

She rang off with her friend and started out to the hallway, but heard another voice in the foyer. A feminine voice. Gui hadn't come alone. And she had a sinking feeling that he'd brought Elvira with him.

Elvira had been crying since he'd come to her house. The media had camped out on her doorstep, and her servants were dealing with them, but Gui knew she needed privacy to grieve. He'd had a call from Montoyes informing him that his brother and sister-in-law were alive, and just a few minutes ago Alonzo had phoned.

He'd talked to his brother and felt deep relief that he was okay. But now he had Elvira in his home and had no idea what he was going to say to Kara. Vincent had a look in his eyes that Gui knew meant his secretary didn't approve. But the other man had been with Gui long enough to know better than to say anything.

"Where is Kara?"

"Upstairs, Count. Should I send one of the maids to find her and let her know you are here and that we have a guest?"

"That's not necessary, Vincent. Please see that Countess de Perez is settled in the Green Room."

"Yes, Count."

"Guillermo, *querido,* you can't leave me," Elvira cried.

"Just for a few moments, Elvira. You'll be fine. Your maid will be here soon. In the meantime Vincent will assign someone to draw you a bath."

"Yes, Count."

"Gui…I need you."

"I know you do, Elvira. And I'll be back to check on you in a few moments. I need to call my parents and make sure they are fine."

"Why should you worry about them? They

haven't lost anyone…I've lost my Juan. How will I live without him?"

Elvira had been asking the same questions over and over again. And Gui had no answers. He felt bad for her. Had felt her pain as she'd cried over losing her husband. He could only guess there was more love between her and Juan than he'd assumed.

But he needed to talk to his mother. He knew that his mom would be upset about Juan and the near miss for everyone else. He nodded to Vincent and went up the stairs two at a time. He entered his den and immediately knew that Kara was there.

Her flowery perfume was a scent on the air. "Kara?"

"Sorry. I came upstairs to take a call from Katie," she said from deep inside the room. He couldn't make out even her outline.

"You're welcome in my den. Why are the lights off?" he asked as he entered the room.

"I wasn't sure what the news would be. Did you hear that Alonzo and the Enfanta are both okay?"

"Yes, I did," he said. He turned on one of the lamps on the side table. She was standing near the desk. Seeing her didn't offer any clues as to what was going on in her head.

"I'm sorry to hear about Juan."

"Thank you. I'm going to call my mother now."

She nodded. "I'll leave you to it…"

"Was there something else?" he asked when she hesitated in the hallway.

"Did I hear someone with you downstairs?"

"Yes, you did. I invited Elvira to spend the night here. Her house was overrun with media and she had only servants at home." He realized he was explaining himself, something that he never did.

"Didn't you think to ask me first?"

"She's grieving, Kara. And she's an old friend. I couldn't turn her away."

"Of course not," she said, walking toward the doorway.

"I don't answer to you. Even after we are married."

"I know that," she said. Her big eyes were wide and she kept blinking. He had the feeling she was fighting back tears and he felt like a total jerk.

But this hadn't been the easiest day for him. And he still had to talk to his parents. And then finish getting Elvira settled in.

"I'm sorry," Kara said. "We can talk about this in the morning. But please remember what we talked about when I agreed to be your fiancée."

"What was that?"

"That neither of us would hold the other to this marriage, or engagement, as the case may be, if the other found love."

He wanted to curse. "I can't deal with jealousy right now, Kara. My family has just had a bad scare and I need to make sure that they are okay. I'll deal with you when I have more time."

She took a deep breath and then walked back into the room, closing the door behind her. She didn't stop until less than a foot separated them.

"First off, I'm not jealous. You told me there was nothing between you and Elvira and I believed you."

"Very well. Then what is this about?"

"This? Gui, you called me over three hours ago and said you'd be home in a few minutes. Your family has called looking for you, and I had to say I had no idea where you were. Then I get the news from Katie that the husband of your old lover is dead, and you show up with her in tow. What do you think is wrong?"

He leaned back against his desk, crossed his arms over his chest. He'd been hoping for the peace that Kara always brought to him and instead tonight he was finding more chaos than he wanted to deal with right now.

"It sounds like jealousy."

"Stop saying that. I'm not jealous. I was worried about you. I thought something might have happened to you, or perhaps you'd learned bad news about your brother and that you needed me, Gui. I was worried because I wanted to be by your side and help you through this."

"I don't need that."

"You don't? What *do* you need then? Because I've tried everything I can think of to be what you need, and I still can't figure it out."

"I need a woman who knows when to give me space. I need a woman who will realize that in the middle of a family crisis, I can't deal with her and her petty jealousies."

"Is that really what you need?"

"Yes, it is."

"Then I guess you don't need me."

She pivoted on her heel and walked to the door, and he let her go.

Eleven

Kara had no idea where she was going to go, but she needed to get away from Gui and away from his house. But he stopped her before she got very far.

"Don't run off like this. I know that my words seemed harsh, but this hasn't been an easy day."

She went back to him, putting her arms around his waist and hugging him. He sighed and hugged her back and she thought that maybe things would be okay. "I know this has been a long day."

"Yes it has."

"What can I do to help you out?" she asked. She was going to ignore the fact that Elvira was in the home that he shared with her. Try to ignore the fact that the woman who'd made her courtship with him so difficult was now sleeping in one of the guest bedrooms.

"Just give me some time to sort everything out."

She drew back from him. "What do you need to sort out?"

"The stuff with my family and Elvira."

"Gui? What are you saying?"

"That she's going to need me."

"Okay. What will she need from you that she can't get from her other friends?"

"We were close, *mi dulce.*"

"I understand that. And you know what? You may have been right when you said I was jealous," she said, realizing that she was going to have to be totally honest with him. Because if he was going to spend time with Elvira, she was going to have a hard time dealing with it. She understood grief, but right now she needed Gui to reassure her. She was almost certain their wedding would have to be postponed, and she really wanted to hear him say he still wanted her.

"I know."

"Gui, I'm trying to have a conversation here."

"I'm trying, too. You mentioned your jealousy of Elvira before, when she sent you that gift."

"That wasn't jealousy. She was trying to undermine our relationship."

He shook his head. "You need to stop thinking everything is about you."

"I'm not making everything about me. But tonight, parts of this are. I think we have to talk about our wedding, because I can't imagine celebrating our lives together a day or two after your family attends a funeral. And that seems like a pretty important thing to discuss, Gui."

"I agree. It is important. I hadn't even thought about our wedding. We should definitely postpone it."

His words cut pretty deep, but then she remembered that he didn't believe in love. God, why couldn't she have remembered that earlier? Before she'd let herself fall in love with him?

"You forgot about it? I think that says everything I needed to hear."

He rubbed the back of his neck and she knew he had to be exhausted from the day. But she wasn't sure where they stood, and she didn't want to go to bed with doubt in her mind.

"I was worried about Alonzo."

She nodded. "I understand. Perhaps we should save this conversation for the morning. I'm tired and upset about everything as well."

"Good idea."

"Can I get you anything tonight?"

"No, thank you. I'll see you for breakfast."

She nodded and left him there. Nothing had been settled between them, and she was afraid to walk away. But it seemed that, no matter what Gui might need from her, what he wanted right now was to be left alone.

By the time Gui showered and changed, he realized he couldn't leave things as they were with Kara. He decided to order a light supper and invite her to share it with him. He headed downstairs to set things up. Vincent was waiting for him at the foot of the stairs.

"Vincent."

"The Countess has asked that you go see her."

"I will. After I have supper with Kara."

"Ms. deMontaine has asked not to be disturbed for the rest of the evening. I believe she has gone to bed."

"Did anything happen I need to know of?"

"Not that I'm aware of."

"Very well. I will go to the Countess."

Gui didn't understand women. And after tonight, he doubted he'd be any closer to that.

He rapped on Elvira's door. Her voice, soft and weak, called out to him. He opened the door and walked inside. It was as dark as his den had been earlier, but this room didn't feel welcoming. He could see Elvira from the light she'd left on in the adjoining bathroom. She was reclining on the chaise longue and had a box of tissues at her side.

Even though she'd been crying all evening, she still looked incredibly beautiful.

"Oh, Guillermo. Thank you for coming back. I'm not sure I can sleep tonight."

He had no idea what to say to her. "I misjudged your relationship with Juan all these years."

"Many people did. It was true that I flirted a lot, but that kept Juan on his toes. And he always made me the center of his world."

Gui could understand that, because it mirrored the relationship they had had years before. Jealousy and passion, the two things that Elvira inspired in all men. "I'm not sure how I'm going to survive without him."

"You will make it. You're a strong woman."

"Yes, I am. Everyone always compliments me on that."

There was nothing wrong with her ego even now, when she was clearly upset. He had a new respect for Elvira, seeing the depth of her grief for Juan. "You really did love him."

She was startled by his comment. Hell, so was he. He hadn't intended to speak out loud.

"Yes, I did." She sat up and patted the chaise next to her. "At first I did turn to him to make you jealous, but he understood me in ways you never tried to."

Gui sat down next to her. "I didn't love you, Elvira."

"I know that. I always have known it. Juan treated me like a queen."

"Exactly as you deserve."

"Every woman deserves that, Gui. Don't you forget it. I haven't been that kind to you over the years… A part of me wanted you to feel the same kind of pain I did when you left me."

"I did," he said.

She shook her head. "No you didn't. You were too full of yourself, and, to be fair, I was, too. We both thought the other would bend. I figured Juan would make you offer marriage. You thought that I'd back off of my demands when you came back."

He shrugged. As he'd said to Kara, this was ancient history. "We weren't meant to be a couple. I think we would have killed each other if we'd tried to live together."

"That's true. I owe your fiancée an apology."

"Why?"

"I haven't made things easy for her. Juan told me to leave it alone but I…I was so jealous that you'd marry her and never even offered for me. I know that I had no right to that. You aren't the right man for me, but I couldn't stand that."

"Why are you telling me this now?"

"Because it caused a row between Juan and me, and now he's gone, Gui." Elvira started to cry again. "And I'm not going to be able to apologize and make up with him. But you still have your lover, and I don't want my actions to hurt another relationship."

Her words made him realize what she was saying. That life was way too short to fight over the unimportant things. She had loved Juan, and Juan had loved her back. That was what mattered.

But he had never believed in love and had the feeling that love was the only thing that was going to make things right between him and Kara.

And he couldn't give her that. He could buy her sports cars and jewelry, but emotions were harder for him. Especially after a day like today, when he realized how painful it was to really care about anyone outside his family.

But one thing he did know was that he didn't want to lose Kara. It was funny that up until this moment he hadn't realized how important she was to him. But compared to Elvira... Well, there was no comparison.

"Are you comfortable in this room?"

"Yes. Thank you for letting me come here to-night. I'll be out of your hair in the morning."

"Where will you go?"

"Back to my home. My sister will be there first thing. I have to start planning the service for Juan…"

She teared up again and he reached out and hugged her to his side. She was too small in his arms. She didn't fit him perfectly, the way that Kara did. And he realized that he was impatient to say good-night to Elvira because he wanted—no, needed—to get back to Kara.

Kara fit him like a glove. Not just during sex, which was important, of course, but also in his life. She softened his rough edges and made him a better man.

And he was ready to start acting like that better man. Like a man that she'd be proud to have at her side. And he owed her a real apology for his remarks earlier. He knew better than to lose his temper. He always said things he regretted. He should never have done it with her.

Kara was the most important thing in his life. How could he not have realized it before?

A few minutes later, he left Elvira and went up-stairs to Kara's room. He opened the door and found the room dark and quiet.

"Kara?"

He heard her quiet breaths. Thinking she was

sleeping, he closed the door and went into his own room, promising himself he'd make up for his surly behavior first thing in the morning.

Running away wasn't really her style, but when Kara saw the news clips of Gui and Elvira leaving her house, soon after her conversation with Gui, she knew she couldn't stay in Madrid. It wasn't enough to just get out of Gui's home. She had to leave the country.

She knew that Gui had only been comforting the other woman, but she could imagine the unkind comparisons between her and Elvira before they even started. And she had enough issues with the way she looked to endure days of unrelenting media comparisons. So she'd made a few calls, packed an overnight bag and asked Vincent to call her a car. She also left a note for Gui, telling him she would see him sometime after Juan's funeral. Perhaps it was petty of her, but she didn't think she could bear watching him take care of Elvira during the funeral and pretend all was well.

She took a cab from the house in the early hours of dawn. The sun was just coming up over the horizon when she reached the airport. She had a ticket to Monte Negro, where she had ordered a yacht several months ago. She would pick it up and then take her time sailing back to Spain. She needed to be alone where she could let her guard down and try to figure out what was going on in her life.

Could she really marry the man she loved when that man didn't love her? A man who could always have women who were prettier and skinnier than she was on his arm?

And was she going to be the confident woman who had stood in front of her lover on the balcony wearing nothing but moonlight, or was she going to revert to the woman she'd always been, that shy and insecure girl who thought that she'd never have a chance to walk down the aisle as a bride in a pretty white dress?

Yet Gui made her feel like she was beautiful and sexy. Not in a way that the entire world recognized, but in a way that happened only between a man and a woman who were meant for one another.

She felt tears sting the back of her eyes. That made her mad. Why didn't he see how perfect they were for each other? They could have a marriage based on feelings so much deeper than the superficial arrangements so many in their social set found acceptable.

Why couldn't he acknowledge what he felt for her?

Her cell phone rang and she glanced at the caller ID before answering. "Hello, Rina."

"Kara, where are you? Gui is frantic. He's been calling everyone we know."

She felt stupid now. She'd ignored Gui's calls because she hadn't wanted to talk to him. Hadn't wanted to hear him tell her again that she was jealous of Elvira.

"I'm at the airport. I needed to get away for a few days. Yesterday was so long, and Gui is dealing with a bunch of stuff."

"Kara?"

"Yes?"

"What the hell is going on with you? I thought you loved Gui. That you were determined to marry him. Isn't that what you told me?"

"Yes it is. But what does that have to do with anything?"

"Everything, baby sister. You can't run away the first time he doesn't act like your knight in shining armor. You aren't living in a fairy tale, Kara. This is real life. It's messy and it doesn't follow a script."

"I know that."

"Then act like it. Go back home and talk to him. Running away has never solved anything, has it?"

"No, it hasn't. But there are some things that even I can't fix."

Rina didn't say anything for a moment and Kara heard the call for the first-class passengers on her flight to board. Was she going? She had no idea. Part of what her sister said made sense. But staying meant dealing not only with Gui and the fact that she'd left, but also with the reporters and Elvira. And she wasn't sure she was ready for all of that.

"Tell me what they are."

"Rina, you can't fix my problems."

"Of course not. But Gui can. I told him he had to make you happy."

"He has."

"He isn't right now."

"What do you want me to say?"

"I want to know what you need to be happy, and then I'll call Gui and tell him to do it."

She almost cried at her sister's words. Didn't she realize that telling Gui what she needed to be happy wasn't the solution? "I need him to figure it out on his own, Rina. If I have to tell him how to fix what's bothering me, then we'll never really be happy together."

"What do *you* want?" Rina asked.

The attendants started general boarding of her flight, and she picked up her overnight bag and moved toward the line of passengers.

"Kara? Don't leave him. Not yet. Go back there and talk to him."

"I can't, Rina."

"Why not?"

"Because he doesn't love me. He doesn't believe in that kind of emotion, and that's the only thing that will make the things he said to me last night disappear. And it would make the things that the media always says about me seem not important.

"But he's not that kind of man, and I've just realized that I am not the kind of woman who can compromise on this. Falling in love with Gui was the most powerful thing I've ever experienced, and to know that he doesn't feel the same way for me…I just can't stay."

Rina took a deep breath. "Oh, honey. I warned you about men like—"

"Please don't say you told me so. I thought you were warning me because I am fat and he'd never fall for a big girl."

"Kara Evelyn deMontaine, you aren't fat and I will not tolerate you saying that."

"Rina—"

"No. Enough of that kind of stupid comment. I warned you off of Gui because I thought he couldn't commit to one woman, and I didn't want to see you hurt."

"I love you, Rina."

"I love you, too, Kara. Be safe wherever you decide to go."

She said goodbye to her sister and eyed the line to board the plane. Was she really going to leave behind the only man she loved?

Twelve

Gui had never lost anything that mattered to him. He'd walked away from Elvira years ago, and when he'd come back, she'd found another lover. He'd made peace with that. He'd used her marriage to drive himself further into the kind of emotional isolation that had always made him feel comfortable.

But losing Kara was horrid. It had been three days since he'd seen her. Yesterday he'd sat with Elvira and his family during Juan's elaborate funeral service feeling a huge hole where Kara should have been by his side. Today the world was going on without him, and he found he couldn't function.

Rina had been absolutely no help in finding Kara, calling him once and telling him that Kara was safe and that was all that he deserved to know.

He'd used his resources and had found her in Monte Negro, but had no idea what to do now that he'd found her. He knew that she would need a big gesture from him. Hell, what she needed was his love and he didn't know if he loved her. Didn't know that he could ever say to a woman that he loved her.

But this wasn't just any woman. Kara was the woman who'd changed his life and made him realize that he had something worth losing. How could one person impact his life this much?

Even his sisters were at odds with him because he'd let Kara slip away. With his family upset with him and having other things to deal with, he had nowhere to turn other than to Christos and Tristan, who'd always had his back.

After two days of drinking on Christos's yacht, the other men were restless to get back to their brides. But the bond of friendship was strong, and they were still here with him.

He took a sip of coffee and stared at the horizon.

"Why did you ask her to marry you?" Christos asked.

He shook his head. He'd sound like a total bastard if he told them his real reason. "I like her."

"Yeah, but you didn't at my reception. You barely knew her. Sheri said she thinks you were afraid that Christos and I would leave you behind now that we're both married."

Gui snorted. "What kind of idiot gets married because his mates have?"

"One that looks like you," Christos said with a laugh.

Gui flipped him off. "I'm not married."

"That's the problem," Tristan said. "You let it go too long. You should have hustled her up the aisle as soon as she said yes."

"I'm not into rushing," Gui said, taking another sip of the strong Greek coffee. These days were endless, and he felt the emptiness of Kara's presence in a way he'd never expected to. How could one woman change his life in such a short time? And why hadn't he realized it before she'd left?

"Liar. You run through life where everything else is concerned."

"Christos, you're supposed to be my friend."

"I am. That's why I'm being blunt. And we don't have the luxury of letting you take three months to decide what to do the way you did with Elvira."

"Well, that worked out the way it was supposed to," Gui said.

"But Kara is different, and so are you when you

are with her. You've done nothing but talk about her since we got here. You need to go after her. Enough sitting here drinking and talking."

"I don't know how to win her back, Tristan. I hurt her. Told her I didn't need her, and then went to comfort another woman."

"So tell her you're an idiot and give her something expensive," Christos said.

"Did that work with Ava?"

"No. But she wanted something else from me."

"What did she want?"

"None of your damned business."

Gui smiled at Christos. He knew what his friend was getting at. This wasn't the kind of problem that could be solved in discussion with his friends. He needed to do something that would show Kara exactly how much he loved her.

Oh, hell, did he love her? Was that why he'd had this dull ache inside his body since she'd left?

"Gui?"

"Hmm?"

"You okay?"

"I think I'm in love."

Tristan spit his coffee out and started laughing. "You say that like it's a bad thing."

"It is, because I have no idea what to do. How to

get her back. And I've just realized that I don't think I can live without her."

"That's love. You know, the bigger you screwed up the bigger the gesture has to be."

"I told her I didn't believe in romantic love."

"You're screwed. She's not going to believe you've changed your mind."

"Unless I do something that proves it beyond a doubt to her."

"Unless you do that," Christos said. "So what do you have in mind?"

He had no idea. Kara was a generous person and she gave so much of herself to everyone around her. He needed to give something to her. Something that she'd never ask for or expect. He needed to prove to her—and to himself—that she was the woman he loved. The woman he wanted to be the center of his world.

And there was only one way to do it, he thought. Only one way to make her believe it. He was going to have to make a big public gesture. And it couldn't just be a gesture, because Kara would sense that and reject him.

He had to really believe in what he did. He had to act from the heart and convince her that she was the woman he loved. The woman he needed in his life. Not just for now, because it was convenient for them to marry, but because she was the only woman he could picture his future with.

How was he going to do that? he wondered.

Kara should have been relaxed after a few days vacationing in Monte Negro, but the island beauty was lost on her. She saw couples honeymooning and lovers everywhere, and it just underscored to her the loss she felt at not having Gui by her side.

One thing she had noticed while she'd been in the seaside town—men were paying attention to her. When she left Gui, she'd taken with her a new confidence in herself. By not staying with a man who didn't love her, she'd realized that she had her own power and her own beauty.

Of course, that realization had taken a few days, but it hadn't been hard to work out. She didn't have to take whatever scraps Gui handed her. She deserved real love. She wasn't the fat sister anymore. She was a beautiful woman who deserved Gui's love.

She wondered if she'd been too hasty in leaving. So what if he'd said he didn't need her? He'd sort of reached out to her again that night. Leaving was a cowardly thing to do. But staying while Gui comforted Elvira wasn't something that she would have been able to live with. Not when he wasn't committed to *her* completely.

She shook her head. Asking her to marry him wasn't enough. Gui had to love her, too. They could have a once-in-a-lifetime love. At least, as far as she was concerned. So letting him go was the stupidest thing she'd ever done.

But going back… She had no idea how she could go back to the way things were. It would give him license to treat her poorly for the rest of their lives together. It would be like saying to him, I love you, so you can walk all over me.

And there was no way she could live with herself if she did that. So here she was, spending her days in a luxury hotel, sunbathing, eating gourmet meals and pretending she was okay when in reality she wasn't.

In reality, she was heartbroken. Wounded from loving the wrong man. And she couldn't even comfort herself by pretending she no longer loved him. She did.

And maybe he wasn't the wrong man, she thought.

Every day, she woke up and hoped that he'd come for her. Which was stupid, because he wasn't going to make that kind of gesture. She wasn't the kind of girl men like Gui chased after. He'd expect her to come back to him. Especially after the way he'd come back for Elvira and she'd moved on. She knew she was waiting for nothing.

She was giving herself time to recover from loving him so much. How did that happen? How had she let herself fall for him when she'd decided to be smart?

She still hadn't found the answers she'd been seeking when she left Madrid. She'd run away, and that was the plain truth of the matter. For the first time in her life, she'd done something irresponsible, and she was struggling with it. She was needed back at her job, and she knew she owed Gui an explanation, but the truth of the matter was she just couldn't face anyone right now.

She had to figure out for herself where her life was heading and why she had fallen in love with a man who couldn't—or rather, wouldn't—love her. It was hard to take. Hard to believe that, for a smart woman, she'd made such a stupid mistake.

Leaving had been stupid. Rina had been right. If she wanted Gui, she should be willing to fight for him. She needed to get herself back to Madrid and let him know what was acceptable and what wasn't. She needed him to be her man. And he'd asked— no, he'd *told*—her to marry him, so he needed to step up and love her as well.

"Ms. deMontaine?"

She glanced at the short man standing next to her table. She'd stopped for lunch at one of the seaside cafés. It was a nice spring day in a paradise, she thought, in this A-grade resort town for the rich and famous. And forlorn.

"Yes, I'm Kara deMontaine."

"I was asked to give you this."

He handed her a large padded mailing envelope. She reached for her handbag to tip him, but he shook his head. "I'll be over there, waiting for your response."

He stepped a few feet away and Kara opened the envelope. A flat box with a green ribbon tied around it came out. She removed the ribbon and opened the box. There was an embossed card on top of the tissue paper. She lifted it out and saw a note from Gui.

Her heart leapt and started beating so fast she was sure she was going to have a heart attack on the spot.

I was a fool to say I didn't need you. You mean more to me than I can say. Please join me for dinner tonight at eight.
Yours,
Guillermo

She looked around. Gui was *here?* But she didn't see him anywhere.

She turned Gui's note over and wrote her

response across the back accepting his invitation. "Please take this back to the Count."

"Yes, ma'am. A car will be waiting in front of your hotel at seven-thirty."

She nodded. She finished her drink and looked back at the box. It wasn't that large, so she ruled out clothing, and it was too big for jewelry.

She pushed the tissue paper aside and saw that it was a book. She lifted it out of the box and stared down at the cover. It looked like an illuminated manuscript from medieval times. On the cover was a knight in shining armor on a horse. The knight was looking up at a castle, and in the tower was a woman who looked at lot like her. She had long, black curly hair like Kara's. And her eyes were gray, just like hers.

She lifted the book up, looking more closely at the knight, and noticed this time that he looked like Gui.

She opened the book and saw that it was the story of Gui and Kara. The book was written just like a fairy tale. Starting with Once Upon A Time…

She flipped the pages to see what happened in the story, reading along. The book was exquisitely made and on each page were hand-painted drawings that depicted another scene of the knight and his princess. Gui must have paid a fortune to have it made so quickly.

But the story ended abruptly when the princess

disappeared. The knight was looking for her—and then there was nothing but blank pages. She closed the book and put it back in the box. She wasn't too sure what Gui had in mind for this evening, but it was clear to her that he had come for her.

And that meant the world. She wished she knew where he was, because she didn't want to waste another second without him by her side.

She paid her tab and left the restaurant, walking up the avenue to her hotel.

Leaving Madrid felt like a hundred years ago. She had no idea what had happened after she left. She felt ashamed that she hadn't followed Juan's funeral in the news. But now she had hope bubbling up inside her. That same hope that she'd felt the first moment she'd realized that she loved Gui.

And there was nothing to stop it. She had never believed she was the kind of woman who would have a great love in her life. It just didn't seem like something that would happen to someone as practical as she was. But Gui had found her, and she had fallen in love with him. And now she was beginning to believe that he loved her, too.

Gui watched Kara from the shadows as she read the book he'd had made. He knew he'd made the right choice when he saw her face light up the second she saw the book and realized that it was their story.

It had taken him three days to get the book made and to get everything in place to come and woo her back into his arms.

He had been a jerk the day of the accident, and a part of him knew that Kara would cut him a certain amount of slack for some of the things he'd said, but when it got down to it, he'd let her go. He'd pushed her away because he'd been afraid of acknowledging that he had deep emotions for her.

Hell, he loved the woman and he was still afraid to say it. Even to himself. Damn, what would he do if he couldn't convince her to come back into his life and marry him?

He followed her into the lobby of her hotel, making sure she was safely inside and on the elevator up to her room before he went to the house he'd rented. He gave Vincent orders to make sure that everything was perfectly prepared for the evening.

At six o'clock their friends and family started to arrive. Kate, Emily and Courtney were friendly to him, a marked difference from two days ago when they'd barely spoken to him. Rina still wasn't sure that she believed he could fix the hurt he'd delivered to her sister.

Christos and Tristan gave him a clap on the back

and wished him luck, and Ava and Sheri kissed his cheek approvingly.

He went in the car to pick her up, and when he arrived at her hotel and saw her in the lobby, his breath caught in his chest.

"Kara."

"Gui."

"You look gorgeous tonight, *bebe.*"

"Thank you. You look very nice as well."

He nodded to her. "Are you ready?"

"Yes. Thank you for the gift you sent this afternoon."

"You are welcome. Did you like it?"

She smiled up at him and he felt lighter than he had in days. How had he thought he could live without this woman? "I loved it."

"Well, you are going to have to write the ending. I'm out of ideas."

"I think you still have a thing or two up your sleeve."

"Maybe one last effort to show you that I'm sorry for my behavior."

"I didn't leave because of the way you acted on that last night."

"You didn't?" he asked. They were outside now. Vincent held open the back door of the Rolls-Royce that he'd rented.

She slid into the backseat, and once he was inside and they were on their way, she turned to him. "I left because I realized I couldn't stay with you and continue to love you when you didn't even want to acknowledge that you needed me in your life."

"I was a complete jerk when I said that."

She shook her head. "I understood you were having a terrible day. And I was a little jealous of the time you'd spent with Elvira."

"She means nothing to me other than a friend. And I can't turn my back on friends."

She nodded. "I didn't mean to imply that you should. It's just that she was… Well, she was responsible for everything between us. And…"

"What?"

"She's beautiful, and a part of me felt like I'd never be able to compete with her. I left partly because of vanity, Gui. I never wanted you to see Elvira and me photographed together and feel like you got stuck with the runner-up."

He caught her shoulders and turned her to face him. "Kara, never say that again. You are the most beautiful woman in the world to me. You. No one else. I can't imagine loving anyone else as much as I love you."

She shook her head. "But you don't believe in romantic love."

"I was an idiot. I think a part of me was always afraid to admit that I believed in love because I never planned to experience it. But with you, I have no choice. I love you, Kara. And I can't live without you."

"Do you mean that?"

"I never say things I don't mean."

"Oh, Gui. You're the man I've always secretly dreamed of finding and having for my own. I love you very much."

He drew her into his arms and kissed her full on the lips. But he was careful not to let their passion get out of control.

They arrived at the house a few minutes later and Vincent opened the door for them. Gui got out first and then reached down, offering Kara his hand. She took it and got out. When she was standing by his side he couldn't resist wrapping his arm around her waist and leading her up the steps of the house.

She hesitated when he opened the door and she heard the voices from the patio area. "Who's here?"

"Only the people who are most important to us. This is an important night and we need our friends and family around us."

"For dinner?" she said.

He heard the hope and the concern in her voice. "A bit more than dinner."

He led her out to the patio, where she was greeted

by her friends. As she was welcomed to the house, Gui went to make sure he had everything he needed for his part of this night.

"You seem nervous," Tristan said, coming up next to him.

"I am. But I know that I need her in my life and I need her to believe how much I love her."

Tristan clapped him on the back. *"Bon chance, mon ami."*

"Gracias."

When Kara was done greeting everyone, he drew her to a platform that he'd had set up next to the pool. Candles floated on the surface of the pool, illuminating the entire area.

He pulled a microphone from his pocket. "Good evening, everyone. Thank you for coming here tonight."

"What are you doing?" Kara asked in a soft voice.

"Something I really should have done back in the beginning," he said to her, then brought the microphone back to his mouth and said, "Many of you know that Kara and I are engaged. And those of you who know me probably already guessed that instead of asking her to marry me, I just told her we should get married. But tonight I want to fix that."

He turned to Kara and got down on one knee. "Kara deMontaine, I love you more than I thought

I'd ever love a woman. Will you make me the happiest man alive and marry me?"

She nodded and sank to her knees in front of him. She threw her arms around his neck. "Gui, I love you so much. I will marry you."

* * * * *

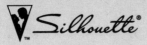

Romantic SUSPENSE

**Sparked by Danger,
Fueled by Passion.**

The Taken

Tierney Doyle is used to being criticized for
her psychic abilities, yet the tough-as-nails—
and drop-dead-gorgeous—detective has no doubt
about what she has uncovered in the case of a
string of unsolved murders. And Tierney is slowly
discovering that working so close to her partner,
detective Wade Callahan, could be lethal.

Look for

Danger Signals
by Kathleen Creighton

Available in April wherever books are sold.

REQUEST YOUR FREE BOOKS!

2 FREE NOVELS PLUS 2 FREE GIFTS!

Silhouette Desire®

Passionate, Powerful, Provocative!

SDES08

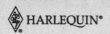
HARLEQUIN®

INTRIGUE®

❧WHITEHORSE❧
MONTANA

No matter how much Nate Dempsey's past haunted
him, McKenna Bailey couldn't keep him off her mind.
He'd returned to town to bury his troubled youth—
but she wouldn't stop pursuing him until he was
working on the ranch by her side.

Look for

MATCHMAKING
WITH A
MISSION

BY

B.J. DANIELS

*Available in April
wherever books are sold.*

COMING NEXT MONTH

#1861 SATIN & A SCANDALOUS AFFAIR—
Jan Colley
Diamonds Down Under
Hired by a handsome and mysterious millionaire to design the ultimate piece of jewelry, she didn't realize her job would come with enticing fringe benefits.

#1862 MARRYING FOR KING'S MILLIONS—
Maureen Child
Kings of California
He needs a wife. She needs a fortune. But when her ex arrives at their door, their marriage of convenience might not be so binding after all.

#1863 BEDDED BY THE BILLIONAIRE—Leanne Banks
The Billionaires Club
She was carrying his late brother's baby. Honor demanded he take care of her...passion demanded he make her his own.

#1864 PREGNANT AT THE WEDDING—Sara Orwig
Platinum Grooms
Months before, they'd shared a passionate weekend. Now the wealthy playboy has returned to seduce her back into his bed... until he discovers she's pregnant with his child!

#1865 A STRANGER'S REVENGE—
Bronwyn Jameson
With no memory of their passionate affair, a business tycoon plots his revenge against the woman he believes betrayed him.

#1866 BABY ON THE BILLIONAIRE'S DOORSTEP—
Emily McKay
Was the baby left on his doorstep truly his child? Only one woman knows the truth...and only the ultimate seduction will make her tell all.